Fifty Shades of Austen
Steamy Secret Diaries of Austen's Naughty Women

By Jane Austen & A. L. Ady

~Acknowledgments~

Thank you to Elisabeth, Ginger, Melody, Rob, Janae, Mallory and Kathryn for all your support.

Thank you Jane Austen, for creating vivid characters and a wonderful world to retreat to time and again.

~Preface~

Fifty Shades of Austen was inspired by a book, but not the one you might think. I found a beautiful 1970's book, bound in powder-blue satin, embossed in gold lettering, titled, *Shades from Jane Austen*, in which the author and illustrator, Honoria D. Marsh, artfully portrays dozens of beautiful silhouettes of Austen's many characters. The title of the book instantly made me think of *Fifty Shades of Grey* by E.L. James, and the parody title *Fifty Shades of Austen* naturally popped into my head.

Having read all the Austen novels many times, I have always been intrigued with the 'bad girls' of Austen, and how they challenged her principled heroines, driving much of the conflict. The stories of these less-than-proper female characters, who surrender to their passions and abandon propriety with equally depraved men, are full of intrigue, desire, and wanton disregard for their family reputations- all for the often short-lived affection of a top-hatted, cravat wearing bad boy. I wanted to know more about these characters.

I wondered, what really happened the night Lydia stole away with Wickham? How did Lucy Steele seduce the brother of her fiancé? Why did unmarried Isabella Thorpe most likely end up in bed with the heir to Northanger Abbey? How did Louisa become engaged to grief-stricken Benwick so quickly? Is Jane Fairfax, who agreed to a secret engagement, really the sweet, quiet, angel everyone thinks she is?

In *Fifty Shades of Austen*, the characters themselves answer the questions through secret diaries detailing every aspect of their romantic desires, manipulative schemes and sensual experiences. Meticulously researched, the details of these character's lives can be followed in Austen's novels, from the settings and social customs, to the carriages and clothing. Each story fits perfectly within the Austen universe. Janeites can have fun tracing the carriages and path taken by Lydia and Wickham on their way to London, or discuss the poetry Captain Benwick would read to Louisa.

I hope you have fun with this wonderful romp celebrating the gloriously greedy, sassy, sexy, brazen, and more-fashionable-than-you women of Austen. These steamy stories will have you cheering for the bad girl.

CONTENTS

LYDIA'S LONGING
Pride and Prejudice

My Dear Diary,

I can scarcely write for being so happy! I cannot believe what has happened. In scarcely a fortnight I have gone from being miserably bored, nothing but the youngest daughter in a family of dull fools, despising everyone, to being the most felicitous and the most accomplished of all of them! I am to soon be married, the youngest! And I have done what none of my sisters has done. I am living in perfect rapture, and my heart bursts with adoration of my lovely, warm Wickham. He is everything a man should be. Handsome, charming, generous, all the girls love him, but it was me he chose. Over all of them. He simply couldn't resist me. And I couldn't resist him. And won't they all just laugh and laugh when I come home married! To everyone's favorite! Oh! The look on that smug Elizabeth's face when she sees his arm wrapped around mine and a ring on my finger! I shall not wear my glove so they all will see it. To think that I know more than even Jane about the real pleasures in life. That I, only sixteen years old, know more about a man than any of them! And what a man I have! So passionate, so amorous. He was captivating, romantic, and fervent in his declarations!

Stay my heart! I have to start at the beginning or I will get all mixed up about it. I was invited to Brighton by Mrs. Harriet Forster and her husband Colonel Forster. Harriet is not much older than I and her husband is very old and fat. Lord! No amount of pin money would make me marry an old, fat stupid man! But I adore him, for Harriet's sake. Luckily for her, he does not pay much attention to what is going on. In Brighton, we were the center of everyone's attention. All the regiment was in and out of the house all day and night. We had such parties and cards and dances. La! Most nights I danced with Denny and Pratt and drank and played Whist until I was so tired I could hardly get myself to bed. I slept most of the days just so I would be able to enjoy the evenings, even as the other ladies had to retire.

And this scheme is what brought me to my true desire… to see Wickham as much as possible. He would come to dinner or after to play cards. I would rush to pour the coffee so that he could come to me. I managed to be placed at his card table often, though sometimes it was more fun not to be at his table but to be across from him, so that I could look at him and he could pretend not to look at me. Then our eyes would meet and he'd smile that smile that made my stomach tighten and my breath catch and all that lovely sensation of flirting. But this was even more than that. I didn't just want to dance, flirt and talk. I began to feel an ache. A desire to be near him unlike anything I had felt with silly Denny or even Pratt (who asked me to dance more than anyone else). Wickham was not a giddy boy. He was a man. A man of manners, conversation, and humor. He was so funny. Oh! Did he make me laugh! But then he would reach out and touch my arm. And every sensation in my body would tremble. He must have seen how I would go from laughing to trembling in a second. How I would be dancing one moment and then suddenly breathless the next.

We loved to sneak touches. What a game! He would pass me in the hall, not even look at me, but his arm would brush against my arm. We sat next to each other one evening. I dropped a card, silly me, and as I leaned over to retrieve it, he did as well and our shoulders touched and cheeks nearly touched! Well, I could hardly say a word after that and I spent the whole night talking about wanting to visit the seaside the next day, hoping he would get the hint. I spent all night writing to Kitty about Wickham and the wonderful time I was having. She will be so jealous, but it is her own fault she didn't make friends with the Forsters and get herself invited.

But I couldn't care less if Kitty was jealous or not. All I could think about was how I could sneak another touch with Wickham. Harriet and I and the Colonel walked to the seaside the next afternoon, just as I had schemed. The Colonel stayed back to talk with some fat old men while Harriet and I continued down to the sand. What a lark! We took off our stockings as we were on the Eastside women's beach and dipped our toes in the sea water! When we returned shortly after, we were so pink from the sea air and laughing that no one noticed how I blushed terribly when I saw Wickham talking with the Colonel. He did get my hint and he had come to see me! He inquired after my health and said the sea air was improving my complexion, just like that in front of everyone! We began walking and as he walked beside me he touched my arm with his elbow and so I tripped slightly and grabbed his arm!

It became such a fun game of ours that we would devise ways of brushing up against each other. We would touch hands when passing cards. I handed him a coffee or tea and his fingers would linger on mine. I even pretended to fall on a stair landing so he could catch me! And catch me he did. He was so surprised when I flung myself from two steps above! He held my waist in his hands and I looked at him with as much feeling as I could show. He didn't let go, but his hands squeezed a little harder. I can't remember exactly what I felt, but it made me bite my lip to keep from making a sound. He lifted me up like I was a feather and then doted on me, insisting that he check to ensure my ankle was not twisted. I never knew that a man's fingers on my ankle would produce such shortness of breath! He insisted I was very ill and he practically carried me back up to the Forster's drawing room, for I mustn't walk. Of course, that night dancing with him was nothing short of delicious. I was confident now of his attentions to me. He never looked at anyone else. And neither did I. Of course, I danced and played cards with others in the regiment, especially Pratt, who generally made me promise to dance with him at the next party before he left for the evening. But that was nothing at all to me. I only thought of Wickham, and when and how I might be able to be closer to him.

Well, the opportunity came rather quickly, as we had all gone on a walk together two days later. Harriet and Colonel Forster were ahead and Wickham eventually came to stand by me in the back. As we walked, our hands kept touching, and with every touch I felt sparks fly through my chest. As our group rounded a corner, Wickham slowed and actually grabbed my hand! It was too much for me, and I should have pulled away immediately but I simply couldn't. He led me quickly off the path and into the trees! Oh! How I had fantasized about this. And now it was happening! Hidden in the trees, he grabbed my other hand in his and brought my hands to his lips and kissed them. Then he said, "Oh how I long to kiss more than your hands!"

I was in so much shock that didn't notice at first he had let go of my hands and he had wrapped an arm around my waist! He pulled me close and my breast was pressed to him. He was warm. And my entire body warmed to it. I lifted my head, my lips aching for his. I didn't care about anything else. What else was there to care about? He pressed his lips to mine and I thought I would lose my head!

How funny now that we have kissed a million times and so much more. But that first kiss was so longed for, so urgent, so secret. We ran back to the path and quickened our pace. When enquired after, I told them my shoe had come unbuckled and I scolded them all for not waiting for me. After that, the hand touching was nothing. We found ways to disappear around corners for quick kisses, though they only took a second.

One night after cards, I excused myself to go to bed and winked at him when no one else could see. I waited for several minutes by the back of the stairs and then he came! We stole away into the gardens and he said that he had also excused himself to retire early and that no one would come looking for him. Once we were far enough away from the house we hid behind the hedges where there was a little stone bench. After laughing for a moment, he leaned in and kissed me, but this time it wasn't a quick rushed kiss. This was a slow, patient kiss. He held my shoulders and then my back and kissed me until I had to breathe. But when I opened my mouth his tongue came inside with the most wonderful sensation! He tasted of smoke and coffee and I wanted more. I pressed my tongue to his lips and he pulled me even closer, taking in my tongue and pressing more with his own. We were mad for each other and my hands were on his arms and his back and then his neck and in his hair. He touched my leg and I near went into a frenzy. I wanted to be so close to him, I was almost in his lap. Finally, he stopped kissing me and with eyes that could never be refused he asked,

"Miss Bennet, I am soon to quit Brighton and leaving you would be my only regret. Come away with me! Come away and we can truly be together, the way we want to be."

I couldn't believe I was being proposed to! What a glorious laugh! I said of course yes, that I wanted him more than anything and I couldn't wait to be his. So he walked me back quietly and said he would make arrangements and contact me. He left me quickly and I hardly remember how I got to my room, dressed for bed or sat at my dressing table. But I wrote to Kitty again immediately. This time I knew she would be jealous for sure. But I also knew she would keep my secret because she knows she is the only one in the world I would ever tell this secret to. I also wrote to my friend in Bath who would get a great laugh in knowing I was secretly engaged!

Well, it was a few days before I even saw Wickham again! It was torture not to hear from him or see him at all. I began to doubt for a moment that we were engaged and then I thought that maybe something horrible had happened to him. I was working up the courage to ask Colonel Forster if some dreadful accident had occurred when Wickham arrived as fresh and sharply dressed as ever. He greeted the Colonel and walked past me without so much as a head nod, but I felt his fingers pull one of the ribbons on my dress and I knew his plans were made. That evening there was a dance, and as it was a Saturday, more than the usual company were present. With such a large assembly, speaking with Wickham was easier than ever. After he finished a dance with an ugly old maid, probably Lizzie's age but far more fashionable and idiotic, he came to me and spoke for a moment about the elegance of the dance and the healing sea air. Finally, after I had teased him a bit about how boring he was now, he laughed and I knew he was teasing *me*! His tone lowered so that even I could scarcely hear him.

"Follow me after I leave. I have something for you."

I became so agitated with excitement that he could no longer stand near me for fear of our being discovered. After a few moments conversation with the Colonel and other old, fat men he gave his leave. I, of course, followed him a few minutes later once another set had begun and no one was paying attention to me. I walked through the hall and into a dark room at the end. I was wondering where on earth I was supposed to go when I was grabbed around the waist, spun around and Wickham was suddenly kissing me violently! He pushed me against a wall as his body pressed into mine. My whole body shook with excitement. He kissed my lips and then licked them, then his tongue ran along my neck and then to my chest where his hands slid down to lift my breasts up to his face. I grabbed his shoulders and he reached down, pulling up my muslin gown! He pulled it up so quickly that the under layer tore, but his hand was pushing in the petticoat and I felt his fingers tickle right between my thighs. Then he pushed himself against me again, this time I felt his hardness as he kissed me, pressing his tongue against mine! God! It was wonderful! I slid my hands down his back and grasped his firm bum pulling him harder against me. He thrusted forward and for a moment we had forgotten where we were and that people were down the hall. The muted music of the piano forte reminded us of the danger and he pulled away, straightening his uniform and smoothing his front fall. I pulled my dress back down, though it was now torn, and smoothed my hair.

He said, "You must get back now, before you are missed."

Taking one more wet kiss, he said, "We shall leave tomorrow evening!" He passed me a tightly folded note and quickly left. I hurried to hide the note in my shoe and returned to the room where the dance set was just ending. I begged Harriet that I should leave immediately. I did dance a couple more dances, Pratt making me promise to dance with him at the next assembly, of course, and then, finally reaching the privacy of my own room, I threw myself upon the bed to read the letter which I leave here in the page to forever remain as a keepsake of our most secret affair. Lord! I can't stop laughing!

Miss Bennet,

I beg you to forgive the manner of our correspondence, as I know you must take no pleasure in receiving a letter in such a way, but I must lay open my feelings once again and impress on you the secrecy that must accompany my instructions.

I must have you. I think of nothing but you day and night and I shall not wait another day. These last weeks have been both diverting and tormenting, all to your credit, for you are the essence of pleasure and teasing encouragement. You have an open heart as I do with passions and a violence of feeling that I believe match my own. I long to hold you and call you Lydia.

Tomorrow, this Sunday evening, once the family retires, I shall meet you just outside the Forster's garden by the little bench where you gave me full reason to hope that you would agree to quit Brighton and be my companion on a journey northward. Carry very little as we must travel swiftly. Bring any objects of value that may be of use on our adventure together. I pray you will meet me or my disappointment will be great.

Yours,

George Wickham

I was up all night laughing, reading the letter over and over, unable to sit still for excitement! I wanted to tell Harriet more than anything, but I knew I mustn't lest she let it slip to her husband and he would prevent the whole delicious scheme!

Northward! I thought that we should travel to Gretna Green in Scotland and be married. I have heard of such adventures but never thought I would ever be the heroine in such a story! I spent the afternoon choosing the clothing I would pack in my small case and determined to wear my blue pelisse rather than carry it and had the most difficult time deciding which bonnet to bring. I had hardly any time to write a letter to Harriet but it was important for her to know that I would need the rest of my clothes sent to Longbourn and to make my excuses to our friends. I thought about telling her specifically not to send word to Longbourn, but thought better of it because if I made her keep the secret she might send a letter immediately for fear of my parent's disapproval. But won't they all be so happy that Wickham was to be called their son-in-law and brother! What a glorious laugh!!

Here is the letter I scribbled- I rewrote it for Harriet on the nicer paper I found in the desk.

MY DEAR HARRIET,

You will laugh when you know where I am gone, and I cannot help laughing myself at your surprise tomorrow morning, as soon as I am missed. I am going to Gretna Green, and if you cannot guess with who, I shall think you a simpleton, for there is but one man in the world I love, and he is an angel. I should never be happy without him, so I think it no harm to be off. You need not send them word at Longbourn of my going, if you do not like it, for it will make the surprise the greater, when I write to them and sign my name 'Lydia Wickham.' What a good joke it will be! I can hardly write for laughing. Pray make my excuses to Pratt for not keeping my engagement, and dancing with him tonight. Tell him I hope he will excuse me when he knows all; and tell him I will dance with him at the next ball we meet, with great pleasure. I shall send for my clothes when I get to Longbourn; but I wish you would tell Sally to mend a great slit in my worked muslin gown before they are packed up. Good-bye. Give my love to Colonel Forster. I hope you will drink to our good journey.

Your affectionate friend,

Lydia Bennet

The whole afternoon took ages! Dinner was so long, everything began to annoy me and the sound of Mr. Forster slurping his soup so slowly nearly made me lose my mind! But the evening went slightly quicker with a small game of cards and I went to my room as soon as I could get away. I dismissed the maid and told her not to return until morning. I hoped she was not suspicious by my obvious separation of clothes and items I planned to pack.

I was soon dressed, had my bag ready and now I just had to wait. I looked out the window constantly for some sign of Wickham. I was shaking with impatience! Finally, the house felt quiet. I crept out into the hall and made certain no servants were around. I placed the note on Harriet's writing desk, knowing she always passed there after breakfast and as quiet as a mouse I slipped out of the house to the gardens. I stood for a moment in the cool night air, feeling a sense of freedom and joy unlike anything I'd felt before. I knew some would think it impulsive or rash for me to hasten a marriage, but why shouldn't I? If we are determined, nothing and no one can stop us and we shall have such a laugh together. Why should we wait ages to be together and have a stuffy wedding full of tiresome people? My father will thank me for avoiding such cost and inconvenience.

I nearly ran to the bench and, finding it empty, I sat and waited. I was growing very cold and for a moment I was afraid he had come and gone! What if he thought I didn't come? Why had I waited so long to leave the house!? But at last Wickham arrived! His warm smile made me forget all my fears and he took my hand. We ran through the garden and to the streets, where there was a hired coach waiting. Without a word, the driver took my bag and then we were off! Just like that! I snuggled up to Wickham and he took my glove off and kissed my hand. He allowed my hand to touch his lovely smooth face, and he ran my fingers over his lips. He kissed each of my fingers and then his tongue licked between my fingers and my whole body went warm! I felt my legs shiver and I pressed myself even closer to him. He said that as soon as we could find a room together we would no longer have to be confined to hand kissing and he placed my hand on his leg! We were soon stopped and

Wickham got out as I hastily replaced my glove. We switched to a chaise that was waiting and headed to Epsom.

It was so exciting, running away with my love who was so faultless and had everything perfectly planned! Such a gentleman I have never known! He whispered in my ear most of the way to Clapham where we switched to a hackney coach. I wasn't paying much attention to where we were going, and it was very dark outside. I became so tired that I leaned onto Wickham and slept, so I was surprised when he woke me and we were in London! I asked if we were going to Scotland tomorrow and he promised to explain everything once we were safe in our room.

We walked for a short while and were soon on Edward Street where Wickham was greeted by his old friend Mrs. Younge, who apparently worked on the Pemberley Estate where Wickham was raised. Imagine having to grow up at that hideous, stuffy estate with the horrible Darcys! My poor Wickham! Mrs. Younge gave us a small comfortable room and Wickham explained that tomorrow we would have our own private lodgings. He explained that we did not need to go to Scotland, we could stay in London and he had something very special planned for us!

He didn't give away his surprise, but I knew it was to be a London wedding! What a dream! It was so late that I should have just laid down to sleep, but I was so excited to be alone with Wickham that I thought my heart would burst out of my chest. He locked the door and turned to me with the most charming smile and eyes full of longing that I knew I couldn't make him wait another moment. We were engaged after all and soon to be married. Why should we wait?! We were mad for each other!

I wasn't sure what to do, but Wickham was the highest of men and did everything for me. First, he unbuttoned my coat and hung it up. Then he took off my gloves and kissed between my fingers with his tongue which made me giggle and practically jump with excitement. Next, he knelt down and removed my shoes. Lord, it felt good to have those off! Then, as if he were a lady's maid, he lifted my dress up over my head and I was happy I had worn my prettiest petticoat and stay. He pulled me close and kissed me. Then, as I opened my eyes, he was removing his cravat, waistcoat and then his shirt! I couldn't breathe. I was simply amazed. He stepped close and put my hands onto his warm chest and I couldn't stop running my hands over his skin and soft hair. How exciting! How bad we were! And yet our love was so pure we were the most innocent people in the world.

He moved behind me and, while kissing my neck, he untied the stay and loosened it well enough to pull over my head. Then he unfastened my petticoat and let it fall the floor. I was in such a rush now that I turned to him to run my hands over his chest and feel his kisses on my lips. He suddenly lifted me up and dropped me down on the bed. I laughed and he quickly removed his trousers and stood before me completely naked! I could not laugh then for I was in total shock. I looked away not sure if I should be looking and comforted myself, knowing we had so many more nights together forever and I should soon grow to not be embarrassed. He moved onto the bed and I held my breath having no idea what was to come next. He kissed me. He held me. He ran his hands all over me. He lifted my chemise up over my head and then laid on top of me. He smiled and I could not believe this was happening to me.

Finally, we came together, and while uncomfortable at

first it was soon quite enjoyable and we were especially quiet so that no one else in the house would hear us. The candlelight made him so beautiful and we sat up together so I could see him and feel him even more. I was just starting to really feel something, like I couldn't get a full breath, a tightening of the muscles in my legs and a warmth and a tickle growing in intensity when he could no longer continue and he abruptly ended it, turning away and releasing all the tension that was built up inside him. I laughed and he shushed me quickly. So I held him for a moment and we both collapsed exhausted in the sheets and pillows.

I knew there would be more. I had felt just a hint of it. There was more to come and we had the rest of our lives to enjoy each other. A few hours later the sun rose and I dressed before he woke. I called for breakfast so that it would be ready for him, and I felt such accomplishment. I had done what none of my sisters had done. At only sixteen too! How jealous they will all be! I would be married to my dear Wickham and I would serve him and make sure he had every pleasure.

I stayed indoors all that day as Wickham left to make arrangements for us. Preparing our wedding no doubt. Everything would be secret and what a surprise it would be. I laughed and laughed imagining Harriet reading the letter, and perhaps even being jealous at my catch! What a fun secret for her to keep!

That evening after supper in our room, we moved to other lodgings provided by Mrs. Younge - what an accommodating woman, and why should she not do everything for my Wickham! I determined that we were not far from St. Clements and wondered if we should be married there!

I asked him how long we should stay here before we

are married, and he just laughed pulling me close. He undressed me first, and I had such fun teasing him completely nude as I undressed him! My how many buttons and fastenings there were! Lord! He had a lambskin covering for himself this time, and he explained it would ensure that I would not become with child. At first, it felt different than before, but the more we moved together the less I felt it, and nothing but pleasure filled my body and mind. I laughed and kissed my Wickham and let him touch and kiss whatever he wanted. His face was so handsome and his smile was so grand. His manner was so encouraging, we played with many ways of pleasuring each other over the course of a few days. I discovered I could feel intense pleasure moving on top of him while tasting his tongue in my mouth and feeling him biting my lips.

Whenever he slept, I just kept looking at his face, hardly believing this was my future. How much better was life to be away from Longbourn, adventuring with Wickham? Of course, we shall have to go to Longbourn after we are married, just so I can see the faces of my poor sisters who are not as fortunate as me! They will be beneath me then and have to walk behind *me* to dinner! Ha! I cannot wait to tell all to mother! Well, not ALL, of course, though I wonder when I will buy my wedding clothes? But I know Wickham has it all planned. He is so good.

I don't mind the waiting. I know weddings take time to plan and being married in London is so much nicer than Gretna Green! Only we have been stuck up in this room for ages, several days, and I haven't been able to leave though I long to go out! But Wickham says we mustn't be discovered quite yet or all our plans might be prevented.

But, oh! Who is that coming to our door? Dear Diary, you will never guess who I am looking at out the window! It is that hideously dull and sour man, Mr. Darcy! What on earth is he doing here? My Dear Wickham must have business with him, no doubt. After all, Wickham was raised with that family, as awful as that connection must be to him. Perhaps Darcy will assist in hastening our wedding with some consideration for poor wronged Wickham! But I am in no hurry. I know that we shall be married in London, and waiting is nothing as long as I have my dear Wickham to share my bed. We have had simply nothing else to do but sleep and eat and well... be as we should be... together as happy as any young married couple madly in love can be. I do not think I shall ever stop laughing!

STEELE SEDUCTION
Sense and Sensibility

Lucy Steele
Journal Entry- The Farrars Brothers

Trapped. That is how I felt. Trapped, being engaged to a man who had no love for me at all. Edward Ferrars loved me once, I know he did. But we were young, and he was so handsome and set to inherit a fortune. And he was passionate! You would not know it from his seemingly shy demeanor. But when we had the opportunity to be alone together, finding empty rooms in the school halls or ducking out of a social dance into the gardens, he would allow me freedom to pleasure him with embraces and kisses. As I had no money, I knew that Edward, the first son of a wealthy family, was my best chance at security.

When Edward started to pull away and I learned of his family's most likely opposition to me due to my low fortune and connections, I was very angry, but determined NOT to lose him. I played to his passions, flattered him, and one evening after a concert, I enticed him to slip away with me and we ran into the nearby woods, laughing. He had had quite a few spirits and he was in an amorous mood. I knew I needed to secure him. Knowing his honorable nature, I was certain that once engaged, he would not rescind. So, in the darkened woods, with only moonlight to give us away, I ran my hands all over him, repeating my love for him and begging him to take me, for I simply could not wait for marriage! I placed his hands on my breast and nibbled his ear, which was always his weak spot. He muttered that 'we must wait, we cannot give in to pleasures before marriage.'

So I opened his trouser fall and placed my hands on him until he nearly fell over with pleasure. I made him promise to marry me, "as soon as we may be allowed, so that you may take me, for I need you so badly, I can't stop shaking!"

He soon agreed to marry me and we kissed as I pleasured him. We exchanged vows of love for each other. The next day, he was a bit apprehensive and he worried that his family would not approve and that they would attempt to force him to withdraw or face disinheritance. Well, that would not do, for he meant to be a clergyman and without his family money, we would have nothing! So we decided to keep the engagement a secret. Little did I know how long this secret would have to be kept.

I realize now I was very foolish to enter into such an engagement that had to be kept secret for years! But did I abandon him when he remained determined to have the low fortune of a clergyman? No. Did I despair when his letters stopped coming? No. Did I become jealous when he did send the looked-for letters, and they contained detailed description and praise of a Miss Dashwood of Norland Park whom he had the pleasure of spending a great deal of time with in Sussex? No!

Well, perhaps a little jealous. And enraged. And determined to no longer sit idly by while some flirty elder daughter of a gentleman stole away my Edward.

So I determined that I should go to Exeter to be invited to stay with my cousin at Barton Park and discover for myself this formidable foe. Elinor Dashwood.

Turns out she is nothing. No fortune. No great beauty. No great talent. No fashion. No conversation. Simple. But my Edward could be so simple sometimes, and I could see how her simple charms and soft smiles might have worked on him. I needed to remind him of his promise and connection to *me*. But it was all very difficult to see him or even write to him. So I did the most natural thing in the world. I contrived to befriend my very enemy to keep her from him. I discovered she was unaware of our engagement, and that nothing more than a friendly attachment had ever been understood between them. But she was in love with him. Any fool could see it.

To dissuade her, I brought her into my full confidence. I showed her all the evidence of our engagement. I was certain this would immediately cause her such anxiety and distress that she would feel ill-used and sever all acquaintance with Edward Ferrars. But I was wrong. This conniving and self-interested, nearly old maid, seemed determined to think no ill of Edward and continued to pretend to be my friend in order to get information from me about him.

The fact that he was engaged did not dissuade her from her pursuit! Miss Dashwood was very cunning. She managed to get out of me when I would be leaving to go to London, and when Edward would be in London, and she even contrived to come and stay while *I* was there, pushing herself into the way of the Mrs. Ferrars, Edward's mother, at the same time that I was among the party! Elinor was always there! Like a dark shadow following me around, watching my every move. But I won out! The Ferrars liked me and couldn't stand *her*! Edward's mother and brother, Robert Ferrars, had some notion of an attachment between her and Edward and they would do anything to prevent that horrid connection! Robert was a plain man, the second brother, but much more fashionable than his brother. He was not kind when speaking of others, but to me, he and his sister Fanny Farrars, were kind and thoughtful. I knew that if I could stay among them for some time, they would accept me and allow Edward and I to be married with no ill will.

I still had not been able to see Edward, as he had not returned to London. His entire family expected him to arrive soon, and I listened closely to letters and any conversations that included information about him. I was certain that once he arrived, I would be able to find moments where we could be alone together, and then I would remind him of his affection for me, even if that meant showing an intimacy only reserved for after marriage. I am not completely unknowledgeable in providing for the pleasures of men, and I was certain it would not take much to bring Edward back to his former passion for me.

And then he came! Walked right in on a conversation between Elinor and myself. And I was not insensible to the fact that he came to visit with *her,* having no idea I was there. He came to visit HER before coming to find ME. Well, that put me out! And I was determined to thwart them from any private discourse. I subtly reminded Edward of his honorable engagement to me, while at the same time delivering a delightful sting to that whiny self- absorbed Marianne Dashwood, who is forever crying about the rejection from a man who was reportedly never even attached to her! Though the rumor is that she thought they were engaged, though he had never actually declared himself! Such immaturity is detestable! So as Marianne was complaining that Edward had not come to see them at his mother's house, I said to her,

"Perhaps, Marianne, you think young men never stand upon engagements, if they have no mind to keep them, little as well as great."

Ha! Marianne was too stupid to notice my slight, but Elinor certainly did, and Edward clearly perceived my meaning to him and he became very uncomfortable. It was everything I had not to smile. Edward became so uncomfortable he did not stay to talk with Elinor at all and quickly made his exit. I left soon after Edward and endeavored to catch him walking in the street. I just happened to have a letter for him that I had written the evening before. I had hoped to deliver it safely to him and here was my chance to put it directly into his hands. He was ahead of me and I kept his blue tailcoat in my sights. At last, he stopped for a moment in front of a pretty park. As he was staring blankly into the flower bed, I caught him by surprise. He started when I addressed him and then he smiled and we shook hands. When he did I pushed the letter into his hand. He placed it in his pocket and we made very innocent talk inquiring after each other's families. We walked a little ways in the park and I quickly told him how kind his family had been and of their attentions towards me. I told him they were not so bad as he had imagined and that perhaps we may reveal our engagement without any fear.

He appeared astonished to hear his family praised (I am sure Elinor and Marianne would have nothing flattering to say), but he winced every time I said the word 'engagement'. I feared that Miss Dashwood might hold more sway on him than even previously suspected. As we walked together through the park, I pretended as if I had no idea in the world that his affections were waning. I whispered to him how much I missed him and I squeezed his upper arm when no one was looking. He looked a bit shocked and pulled away softly, but when we were to part, I walked by him so closely that my hip touched the front fall of his trousers. I was certain he would not forget that soon! Now, I only needed time with his family so that we would meet more in common society.

Fortune came, as my sister and I were invited to stay with Mrs. Ferrars and her daughter, Fanny! We were having such a wonderful time, I was certain that another few weeks would ingratiate me into their society so fully that it would only be natural for Edward to be in love with me and that no objection would be voiced. But, alas!

My stupid, imprudent sister goes and reveals the entire affair to Fanny, believing that she would be my ally! And then I thought that was the end of it! We were immediately censured and kicked right out of the house. Servants gathered our things, the chaise was called for us, and we were sent out with nothing but the most harsh words against my person!

I fumed and nearly struck my foolish sister for ruining my plans! Now I could only wait and find out what would become of Edward. My chief fear was that he would break with me in a most dishonorable way. And my next worry was that he would honor our engagement, but he would be stripped of his family fortune, which is one of the enticements that made him so attractive!

Well, proud man, he did stand by me and he did lose everything. His entailment was given to his younger brother, Robert, making him very wealthy. I knew that I should not want to marry Edward now. He was to have nothing to live on until he was ordained and given a parsonage, which could take ages! But I had reason still not to break the engagement. Though he offered to let me out several times (as he was honor bound to do now that he was dreadfully poor), I never relented. I was not going to give Elinor Dashwood the pleasure of having Edward free! His family might still be worked on. And it was this determination that led me to my present happiness.

Edward's brother, Robert Ferrars, came to see me at Bartlett's Buildings in earnest to persuade me to break my engagement with Edward. But seeing him again, this time alone, and viewing him as the fortune's heir, he rose in estimation for me. Here was a new challenge, to make Robert Ferrars admire me, so that he would be on his brother's side and help with the reconciliation. I entreated him to talk with me more. After a few meetings, we rarely mentioned Edward's name and talked mostly of Robert's life, his love for fashion and society, and his hatred of his mother. I listened in earnest, wearing as low cut a dress as I could get away with, agreeing with everything he said. Watching where his eyes would go as I leaned forward to listen to him, I began to discover that his feeling toward me was not mere admiration, but desire. This younger brother always was envious of whatever Edward had and I wondered how I might use this to my advantage.

I tested out my power when I asked him a question and leaned forward, touching his leg. He could not answer straightaway. So I accidently spilled some tea on my glove and had to remove it quickly, as it burned my skin. Robert asked if I was in need of assistance, but I sucked on my burned fingertips and blew on them slowly and said I felt much better. I told him he may inspect the burn and give his opinion of the damage, so he took my ungloved hand in his and I moved closer, so he could examine my hand. I gasped a little at his touch and he was worried he'd hurt me, but I assured him I was not hurt and that the warmth of his hands was a remedy. He held my hand then and even blew on my fingers! I felt my stomach tighten and my legs tingle and quite like that, I was the one being seduced! I wanted more of his hands and more of his breath.

He came to see me every day. I flattered him in ways that would have made Edward color and I worked upon him to make him believe that he was the one now courting me, that he could steal me away from his brother if he tried. I was determined. It was great fun and I thought less and less about Edward while every evening was concerned with how to secure Robert. And I knew Robert's defiant nature. While Edward would defy his Mother only to uphold his honor, Robert would do it out of spite. I allowed him to speak of his mother openly to the point that he said he would love to see the look on her face when he did not marry the favored rich Miss Morton.

This was my opportunity. Here was my chance to secure the fortune that was once promised by the elder Ferrars.

I said, "But then, who would you marry? For any woman would be so very fortunate, in fact humbled and grateful, for you are the most handsome and kind and intelligent man I have certainly ever known."

You may think that was over-the-top, but not so for Mr. Ferrars! He was enraptured by my speeches and when he took my hand, I made a show of great pleasure and guilt in his touch. He expressed the desire of seeing me again, and though I censured him for such behavior, I quickly consented to meeting with him in secret, in a secret place, where we might be more open with one another. So a note came for me the next day with an invitation to a card party at such and such hall, so with that excuse I went and found Robert waiting with a chaise. We quickly left without going in and he drove us in silence to a secluded area near the woods.

I admit I was fearful. I was beyond any protection and even one witness would have ruined me forever, but I maintained decorum and control and teased Mr. Robert Ferrars for bringing us out to the middle of nowhere-how dare he! I took the reins and pretended to take the chaise back myself. It was then that he apologized and professed he only wanted to be alone with me for a moment, to declare his passionate love and that if I would break with Edward, I could be his.

I began with protests (for it would not be much of a conquest for him if I had not put up a fight). I, of course, told him that regardless of my ardent feelings and desires for him, I would never risk him losing the favor of his mother, which she had so recently bestowed upon him. He didn't care a pinch, and said his mother would be mad for a very little while and then relent. She always does.

This gave me confidence that Robert would not submit to living in a tiny parsonage house with no living income and expect me to be happy. Robert's heart was not so deep as to truly love anyone else, as long as I kept a close watch over him. I flattered him for his bravery in risking his mother's anger, but then spoke of Edward and said though I did not have feelings for him as strongly as they once were, I felt bound by my honor. Then Robert said something I had not expected. He told me the truth of Edward's deceitful behavior in how he met the Dashwood sisters while visiting John Dashwood and Fanny at their estate in Norland Park. How the Dashwood girls stayed long beyond their welcome and how Edward had become attached to Miss Elinor Dashwood, spending all day every day at her side and staying long beyond *his* welcome. Fanny had to pull him away just when she felt he was going to make a declaration to Elinor! While still engaged to me! The rascal, the rogue! I could not believe it! I was overwhelmed with anxiety to hear of such dreadful behavior and fell into Robert's arms. He held me for some minutes until I looked up at him with as much passion and meaning as I could portray, with even a tear running down my cheek.

His compassion was great and he kissed me gently, which I returned with more strength. I then allowed him to kiss me fiercely and deeply. (Edward would have never done that!) After a short while I made him return me to the party and we parted with the full understanding of complete secrecy. My sister and his family would never hear of it until we were wed. So we met several more times, each meeting in a private secret place, where we could hold and touch each other and kiss so much as to keep conversation very brief. We, of course, wanted to do more, but I maintained myself, for this was my one allurement now to ensure marriage. I continued to give him pleasure as I spoke and I convinced him that I simply couldn't wait to have him much longer and we had better get married before Edward finished taking orders in Oxford. Robert, in a fit of desire, agreed to marry as soon as we could escape and go to town. So it was settled on the next day.

We were married in town in the afternoon and we instantly set out for the Inn. Clearly Robert was no novice in the way of love making and he took his time to ensure my every pleasure in our wedded bliss. Though not as handsome as Edward, he was not unpleasant to look at and I discovered that I much enjoyed ordering him about as much as he indulged in submitting to it. After our supper and returning to the marriage bed, I placed his hand on my breast and told him that I could give him no stronger demonstration of my love than to allow him all the freedom he could desire. He became so excited by this notion, that I knew he would not regret his choice and would defend me to his mother and do whatever I told him to do in matters of his family and fortune. In truth, Edward never interested me physically. I was not aware of the importance of physical attraction until Robert held me with such strength and kissed me with such passion. We were unremorseful, going against the stuffy social restrictions. Edward was too good, too reserved ever to have been so open with me.

We explored each other until we exhausted ourselves and slept in very late the next morning. We set off to visit my family in Dawlish and passed through Exeter, not very far from where the Dashwood sisters lived at Barton Cottage. It was then that we came across a recognized servant, Thomas, who I knew would be able to communicate news to them. It was so perfect!! He remembered my name, "Greetings, Miss Steele." I had to correct him of course, "I am now Mrs. Ferrars." I asked him to relay the news of my marriage to Mr. Ferrars (I did not mention his first name) and send my compliments to Mrs. Dashwood and her daughters. I even said we should wish to come visit them in the future! Ha! They would be so surprised! Not only would they think that it was *Edward* to whom I was married so soon, but they would also believe that he purposefully slighted them--it was all so funny! They should soon learn the truth of it all, but I hoped they would remain shocked and indignant for quite a while.

I was in such great spirits that I wanted to send letters to everyone I knew. But my first must go to Edward, with whom I was now so angry, for making me stay in a long engagement when his heart was elsewhere! I hated the thought of him wishing to be with that devious, deceitful girl, Elinor. What was she? Nothing! And they would have nothing and be poor and miserable. So let him have her. He had behaved notoriously ill towards me and I should let him know it! Now that I had married his brother, perhaps that would teach him that he did not deserve the fortune he was born to inherit. Now I shall have everything that it would have been in his power to give. Reconciliation with Mrs. Ferrars would take nothing but time and flattery. Robert and I should have every comfort we desire. Isn't it lovely how everything turns out so fortunate for all those deserving?

ISABELLA'S INDUCEMENT
Northanger Abbey

Diary of Isabella Thorpe,
Bath, Spring

Men are worthless scoundrels and rogues. Villains every one of them. They care about nothing but their egos, their pride and mostly their lustful debauchery! The immoral self-indulgence of men knows no bounds!

I could have been the happiest creature in the world, but now I am the most miserable girl who ever lived!

First off, I was engaged to Mr. James Morland, brother to my good friend, Catherine, whom I loved more than anyone! Well, he had presented himself as a man of fortune that would have a generous father and a secure living. Only after we became engaged did he reveal that he would only be given four hundred a year and he would not receive that living for two and half years, forcing us to wait that long to marry! And here I was imagining that I would be within a few weeks saying goodbye to all of dreary Putney, riding in my own carriage and showing off my new ring to all of Fullerton!

Well, I started to try and imagine my life as Mrs. Morland, but with James gone for so long and my disappointment in the situation so great, I was having an extremely difficult time. Of course, to Catherine, I was perfectly blissful. I did not want to betray my apprehension to her at all. I still held hope that the situation might soon change and James' father might do more to allow us to marry sooner.

But that was before I saw Captain Tilney. He was a tall, fine looking man, very fashionable, with a strong chin and dark eyes. Every woman he passed turned to look at him. I watched him speak with my friend Catherine and her constant companion, the annoying Mr. Henry Tilney, his younger brother! I watched as he wandered the rooms, circled the crowd; circling me, in fact. He kept staring at me, and the more I tried to look away, the more I felt his eyes on me. Then he disappeared as the first dance ended and I feared he'd gone. I wondered at myself, feeling attracted to a man when I was engaged to another. I never imagined that could happen. But here I was feeling disappointed that a perfect stranger had left the room. Then I saw him speaking to his brother and even to Catherine again! He left them and came straight towards me. I tried to hide my face until I could push my smile away.

He approached me. He asked me to dance. And of course, I said no. I had told Catherine I wasn't to going to dance that night, as I was engaged to her brother. Also, he seemed the sort of man who would only be interested in a girl who refused him. He pressed me and I begged him to excuse me, and get some other partner. But no, not he. He said that after aspiring to take my hand, there was nobody else in the room he could bear to think of. It was not that he wanted merely to dance, he wanted to be with *me*. Well, I was not at all enticed by his flattery, but after such a public display of persistence how could I refuse him again? It would be best to just placate the man, yet show him no gratitude for the honor or allow him any flirtation.

We danced the whole set together and every eye was jealously upon us. He spoke to me briefly of his swift rise to Captain and his father's secluded estate at Northanger Abbey. I chided him for boasting, so he then switched to telling me that my eyes were lovely and that there was no prettier girl in the room. He began to make fun of all the envious girls in the room who wouldn't leave him alone and who looked as though they wanted my head upon a post! I laughed and enjoyed the dancing exceedingly. He asked me why I refused him earlier and I playfully replied that perhaps my affections were previously engaged. Captain Tilney leaned in close and whispered, "There is nothing people are so often deceived in as the state of their own affections."

And I began to think he was right. Was I really in love with James? Did he really love me enough? After all, he didn't seem to care that we would have to wait over two years to marry and then on so little!

I, of course, explained myself to Catherine immediately after the dance, for she appeared absolutely scandalized! Simple Catherine was easy to pacify with throwing the blame all on Captain Tilney for being wretched. I did not disclose that I planned to meet again with Tilney.

His attentions were constant. Everyplace I went, he

seemed to be there. He would tease me by approaching and then passing by without a word, or joining my party, flattering me with some silly thing about my dress or my hair and then leave again. In the Bath pump-room, he brazenly approached and joined Catherine and me without being invited. Then he proceeded to tease me with wishing my heart was free and some audacious remark about my cheeks. Catherine heard it all but I am sure she did not understand it. She soon left with Mrs. Allen and finally, Tilney and I were sitting alone. He quickly turned to me, his face so close I could feel the heat from his breath. His hand touched my knee under the table and I nearly jumped!

He said, "You love to play games as do I, but I would have you in an instant if you were willing. I will not stop thinking of you and I will see you every day you are in Bath. You shall not be able to escape me. And you may call me Fredrick. No one else can hear."

He left me then and I was in shock for quite some time. A Captain! Heir to a fortune! Would have me if I was willing! Meaning, break my engagement with James and he would propose. I was flying!

Catherine, to my immense surprise, had been invited by the elder father, General Tilney, to accompany his daughter and the younger Tilney brother to stay at Northanger Abbey! So all of the Tilney family left Bath and I was frightened that Fredrick would go with them. But he stayed, apparently against his father's wishes, and I knew it was all for me. When Catherine and the Tilneys were gone, it was much easier to meet with Captain Tilney during the day to exchange a few funs quips, a touch and a glance. I was certain he would propose any day! Then James returned to Bath.

He was just as handsome as ever, attentive and all smiles. I smiled as well but tried to imagine waiting over two years to marry and on so small an income. Still, I had to be secure in Fredrick Tilney's affections before I could break with James. Captain Tilney kept his promise. He was there all the time, despite James, joining our party, scarcely even acknowledging anyone else was there. He was introduced to James and hardly looked at him before engaging me in conversation. I knew I had to be careful, but anytime Tilney came near, I simply lost my head and could not keep from smiling. Poor James started to feel neglected a bit, but in Bath society he cannot expect me to entertain him at every moment. Over the course of the week, James hinted at my partiality for Captain Tilney but I just laughed him off. I just wasn't ready for our confrontation yet. It would ruin all my fun in society. At least not many even knew that James and I were engaged. Only our immediate acquaintances were aware of the connection.

One evening at the theater, I was wearing a fashionable turban and Fredrick appeared behind me, telling me how becoming it was and how every eye in the room was upon me. He bid me to meet with him later and I flatly refused. However, after James and the others had gone in for a smoke after the play, I walked out to find Fredrick waiting. He saw me, smiled, and walked around the corner of the building into a side street.

I hesitated for a moment. My only concern was being seen. But there was no one out on the street. Everyone was inside and after all, I would only speak to him for a moment. I followed him.

The thin alley was dimly lit and Fredrick waited with his back leaning against the wall. I approached, stood in front of him, and waited for him to speak. He wrapped his arms around my waist pulling me against him.

"How you tease me!" he whispered harshly. "How can you make a man so desirous? You are like the water in the mirage and I am the man dying of thirst! When shall I have you?" He leaned in towards me and kissed my forehead. He leaned further and placed his lips on my neck and then he moved to my lips and only slightly brushed his lips against mine. I trembled with excitement, for here was proof of his adoration! I breathlessly promised him, "You may have me, but first I must unbind myself from this hasty engagement." He smiled and pressed his lips fully upon mine, his hands lowering from my back to my hips and around to my backside, pulling me closer to him. He abruptly let go and walked away. Obviously he was afraid he wouldn't be able to control his passions if he kept going. How exciting! When I returned to the house, the men had already come into the drawing room with the other women and all eyes were on me. I hastily explained I only went to get some air. James was silent until I left to go to bed.

The next day, I waited for James and prepared for what I had dreaded. I consoled myself that I was saving us both from a painfully long engagement and a disappointed marriage. I would not be happy on four hundred pounds a year, no matter how handsome the man. James arrived and he was already despondent but I was quite discomfited. I truly did not think it would be so unpleasant and distressing to break off the engagement. I explained that I was unable to continue the honor of our engagement and that he could have no doubt as to the man that held my affections. I assured him of my adoration for Catherine and respect for his family. He seemed not to understand what I was saying, his looks incredulous. When finally he spoke it was so choked, I hardly understood him, but I think he was glad I had been honest in the end. He agreed that continuing the engagement based on my feelings would be offensive to us both. And then I left, unable to bear his wretched face.

Leaving the room, a wave of relief washed over me. It was like the cage door had opened and this little bird was free! I prepared the whole next day for the evening party at the Bath Rooms and had no doubt who I would meet with and how the evening would end. My mother came up to speak to me at one point, and she seemed upset that I was going out so soon after breaking my engagement to be married. But I assured her not worry, and hinted that an even better proposal awaited me. I joined my friends before entering the dance and they all seemed very concerned that I was perhaps saddened by James' immediate removal from Bath to Oxford. I informed them that James and I had mutually broken and it was for the better of us both. They continued to speak to me in worried empathy, but I could not listen. All my attention was in seeking Captain Tilney and finding a chance to be alone together.

And then, there he was, looking as dashing as ever. He was smiling even before he saw me and when our eyes met, he left his friends and came to me immediately. He took my hand without speaking and led me away. I looked back at my friends and they stood gaping at me, clearly amazed and jealous that I had procured such a man's heart. Instead of the dance floor, he led me up the stairs to a hall I had never before been in. I asked him where we were going and he replied, 'A private place, just for you and me.' He smiled at me knowingly, and my heart jumped. He was going to propose this very night! We went into a room and once inside he shut the doors and locked them.

It was a bedroom. An opulent one filled with lavish furniture, including a large bed. He turned to me, his eyes full of desire and he took my hand. He kissed it and said, "Now, may I finally have you?" I nodded eagerly as visions spun through my head of being mistress of grand Northanger Abbey with carriages, barouches, fine gowns, and glittering balls. He kneeled before me. I had always dreamed of a proposal like this, and I felt as if I could not get enough air, though my chest was heaving. He kissed my hand again and he said I had beautiful hands. Long fingers, like my long legs. Then he ran his lips up my fingers and then he kissed the space between them and his tongue flicked up and down. He placed his whole mouth there and gently bit my skin, running his tongue and lips around in a circle. My body warmed and my face literally felt numb from the rushing blush. He looked up at me and told me he wanted to do the same to my long legs.

He slipped off my shoes, stood, and lifted me gently onto the bed and before I knew anything he had my muslin gown and thin petticoat up over my knees! He kicked off his boots and moved his body between my legs, rubbed his hands over my stockings and up to my thighs. The feeling of my legs against his stiff Captain's dress coat was exhilarating. He continuously assured me that he would take care of me, and that he would bring me pleasure I had never imagined. He unfastened my stockings and pulled them off. Then, as I watched with hungry eyes, he fluidly removed his dress coat, cravat, and waistcoat, then finally he pulled his linen shirt over his head. His hands ran over my toes as he kissed my ankles. He slowly kissed up my legs switching from leg to leg. I propped myself on my elbows to watch him and quivered with nearly every kiss. He held my knees and pressed his chest up to my leg. I couldn't resist. I reached forward and ran my fingers over his muscular chest and down to his hard stomach and down to… I pulled my hand back.

I realized that he was fully aroused. Though once I had a friend who explained things to me about men, and how they rose and stiffened to have relations, I really had no idea what to expect. Then he lifted my muslin gown up over my head and crawled around behind me, to untie my stay and unbutton my petticoat with only my chemise left on. Was I really going to do this? Not wait for our wedding night? Perhaps he was not going to fully consummate our relationship now, we were just playing around. I know that many engaged couples play around without fully engaging in sex. His pants were still on after all.

Then I felt his lips between my legs and all rational thoughts left me. My hands were in his soft hair as he licked my inner thighs, pushing my chemise up higher around my waist. My breathing became more and more rapid as he came closer and closer to the most intimate part of me. He paused and I could feel his hot breath on me. Then I felt the warm, wet touch of his tongue. Slow at first, and then fast. A sudden jolt shot up my body and I had never felt such pleasure. I gasped out loud and could feel his smile.

He then sat up and I felt his hand slide up my thigh. His fingertips entered me and he told me to lay back. I did as he said and he gently pressed his fingers into me, slowly moving backwards and forwards until I moaned with pleasure, which urged him move his hand faster and push his fingers deeper. I had my eyes closed, just giving in to the sensations. My whole body trembled and pleasure waves took over my body and mind. I don't know how he did it, but he must have unbuttoned his breeches and unfastened his stockings with one hand because just as he whispered to me that I 'was ready' and he pulled away from me. I looked up to find him dropping his breeches and sliding up between my legs again.

Now I knew what he was about. We were not going to wait until marriage. Would I have waited two and half years with James to be with him in bed? Surely not. I have heard of many couples secretly engaging in relations before marriage. Should I tell Fredrick we need to stop and wait? Oh how it would disappoint him!

He kissed me again, his fingers sliding down around my legs and thoughts of stopping were cast aside. His hands moved up my thighs to my waist, and then up to by breast. His hands lingered there for a moment and then he pulled my chemise over my head. Now we were completely bared to each other. He pressed his chest against mine as we kissed and then he lowered his lips to my breast. His fingers were again inside me as his tongue caressed my breast and it was pure ecstasy! He took my hand and placed it on his lap and I felt how hard and large he was. I could not think how it was possible that he would fit inside me! He kissed my lips again, removed his fingers and then moved on top of me. His body felt so warm and he slowly pressed himself within me. I took a deep breath in as I felt him fill me up. It was uncomfortable at first as he moved deeper within me, but he slowly moved and the sensations of pleasure returned.

After a moment, he began to increase his rhythm and soon we were moving so quickly I thought I wouldn't be able to breathe. I held onto his strong arms and shoulders as he moved above me. He suddenly stiffened and moaned. Then, it was over, and he removed himself from me, leaving me feeling empty and wanting more. Captain

Tilney lay next to me for a few minutes as we caught our breath. He stood to retrieve a towel for me and for himself. He did not speak a word. I watched him as he dressed. Suddenly, I realized he was going to leave the room! I pulled on my chemise and sat up on the edge of the bed. He looked at me and I held my arms open, longing to feel his arms around me again and hear him whisper into my ear. But he turned away, shaking his head. I felt a cold shiver run down my spine and fear ran through me.

He never expressly asked for my hand in marriage, though he implied it. He had bent down on his knee, but he only kissed my hands and removed my shoes. He had said he wanted to 'have' me, not 'marry' me. I held back my panic. I remember exactly what I said, though now I feel like such a fool; 'Fredrick, my darling, we are engaged, of course?'

I shall never forget his cold reply as he pulled on his boots. 'Miss Thorpe, I advise you not to be seen as you return downstairs to your friends.'

He then smoothed back his hair with his fingers and walked out the door. I sat in shock for some time and heard people walk by. My alarm was great as I jumped to turn the key in the lock. I looked around hastily for my clothing and had a difficult time putting them on myself. I felt sore, but my physical pain was nothing to my absolute embarrassment and shame. I had been disgraced, dishonored and humiliated. I had been flattered into idiocy. I had thrown away genuine affection, a real prospect for a future for absolutely nothing! I was ruined!

After I was dressed and had straightened the bedding, (I would not want to be the maid that found this in the morning) I tentatively looked into the mirror over the dressing table. I was shocked by my appearance. My hair was a complete mess and with no comb or brush I could not get it back to a presentable state. I opened all the drawers in the dresser and luckily found a silk scarf that I wrapped around to form a fashionable turban. I knew I had to sneak away without my friends seeing me and then tomorrow make excuses about feeling ill and leaving early.

I waited by the door until I was sure no one was coming. I turned the key and quickly moved out of the room, closing the door behind me. In seconds, I was across the hall and down the stairs. There was no one around. I calmly walked down the stairs and hid my face with my hand as I walked along the edges of the crowded social room to the doors leading outside. Once outside, I made my way around the side of the building out to the main street. At last, I was safe. Walking home was torturous, as I was not only in physical discomfort but full of disappointment, regret, and questions. I even tried to reason that we were actually engaged and he could not rescind. I would hold him to it! Then I argued with myself that I had no proof and anything I said would only discredit me, not him. I reached home and ran straight up to my room. I dismissed the maid after she had brought up fresh water and linen, and undressed, realizing that I was in great need of a bath. But it would have to wait until morning, so all I could do was hand wash with a wet towel and brush out my hair. My hands shook, I was so anxious.

Did anyone see me? Did anyone know where I had been? What excuse should I give? What would I tell my mother if any rumor reached her ears? What of my father? I threw myself down on my bed and cried. I cried for hours. When I woke up it was late. I realized with horror that the maid had already gathered my clothes to wash them. What if she suspected something? I dressed and put up my hair and went downstairs to greet the world. I walked into breakfast and most everyone was finished. My brother yelled at me for sleeping in. My mother smiled and my father didn't look up. So far, all was normal. After breakfast, I panicked when my mother approached, clearly wanting to talk. But it was only about James again. Now I told her that I may have made an error in my talk with him the other day and perhaps James was mistaken about what I may have said. Perhaps if I could speak with him, I might still put things to right. She gave me a look that indicated the matter was hopeless and I ran back up to my room. I had a bath prepared and stayed in it until the water was frigid.

I knew I was expected to be in the Bath pump rooms but I was even more sore this day and could not think of walking and dancing. I made my excuses that I was ill and that would fit with my story of having left the dance early last evening. The next afternoon I did go out. I had to know what people might know. I was prepared for people's looks and being disregarded by my friends. But no such disdain was shown. My friends asked if I was feeling better, and the crowd ignored me. I had concealed it! No one knew and to the world I was still a maid!

That evening I sat down, determined never to dance again, when Captain Tilney walked by with Charlotte Davis on his arm! If my eyes could have thrown knives they would both be dead. I tried not to look as they danced and he so shamelessly ignored me. My friends noticed it and wondered. I flippantly replied that any man may dance with whomever he chooses and it is nothing to me.

I talked to them of James and how my illness had brought reflection and perhaps James and I had a misunderstanding. I told all who would listen of my love for James and my hope that he would return so we might again understand each other. I hoped the rumors might reach him somehow in Oxford, that I wanted to speak with him again. I implored my brother to go speak with him but he refused to leave Bath. I wanted to just stay home but I knew I was expected out and could not change so completely my behavior as to suddenly be unsociable. The next evening, again Tilney was with Charlotte Davis and I began to wonder if she was his next target. But I was told he left the next morning to join his regiment and I was so relieved he was gone. I tried to play that everything was just as it had been and refused to be teased that he was gone. I went to the theater this evening, just to show everyone that I was not going to shut myself up because Tilney had gone or because James had left me. But I wore purple, which is James' favorite color. I shall write tomorrow morning to his sister, Catherine, my dearest friend, at Northanger Abbey. She might have heard rumors there, but I know she will help me speak with her brother and put everything to rights. She is sweet, though rather stupid and uncultured, but she has a good heart and would never suspect any wrongdoing on my part. She will write to James for me and everything shall be as it was. Though four hundred a year is quite a small sum, I am sure his father will be able to do more, by and by.

MARIA'S ABANDON
Mansfield Park

Journal Entry
February- Winter and Wedded.

I am married! Miss Maria Bertram is now Mrs. Rushworth. And I could not be more wretched. I have been married for three months and cannot but regret my choice and my current situation. I cannot declare to anyone my true feelings as I have no real friends that are not connected to either my family, or to my husband, Mr. Rushworth. I spend all day in idleness, with nothing to employ my time, nothing to engage my thoughts, no place to go and no one to see. Mr. Rushworth thinks that I should be content just to be comfortable in lavish surroundings with servants always in the room to bring me anything I desire.

Maybe I should be. After all, isn't that why we marry?

Isn't that why we seek the best match with the best income? So we can all live idle, command servants and be terribly bored with our lives?

If my days are languid, my nights are a torment. Mr. Rushworth is a most passionless man. His only pleasure is in pleasuring himself with no thought to my comfort. His touch is repulsive to me. I had not been physically attracted to him before we were married, so I don't know what I expected. I had only ever felt physically enticed by one man, Mr. Henry Crawford, who treated me so terribly after I thought he felt a serious connection! But after Mr. Crawford, how could I suddenly be excited by or feel pleasure with a chubby, short, clumsy man, completely ignorant to what a woman desires. I dread his coming to my room and I avoid him as often as I can in the evening, and if I cannot, I force myself to drink extra wine.

My only delivery from this nightly torment mixed with this daily mundane lifestyle are letters from my friend, Mary Crawford, whom I hope to soon call my sister, though my obstinate brother, Edmund, still claims an ambition for a profession in the church, which makes it difficult for Mary to accept him with so small a fortune. Henry Crawford sends messages through Mary as well, reminders of our days together in the theatrical, now such fond memories, if only my father had not spoilt it!

Henry and I had grown close during that week rehearsing a play, and though I was already engaged to Mr. Rushworth, I felt such a strong connection with Mr. Crawford that I simply could not restrain it! In the theatrical Lover's Vows, we played the lovers Agatha and Fredrick, and diligent in our rehearsing, we spent many hours together perfecting our lines. During this time I was unsure if Mr. Crawford was only acting or if he might have felt as I did, desiring to make our characters real, to touch more than we might be allowed. We hid ourselves away so we would not be disturbed, but really we did not want my fiancé, Mr. Rushworth, to come upon us.

We acted in earnest, looking at each other with passion, needing our books no longer. Henry, as Frederick, professed his love over and over again, taking my ungloved hand and bringing it to his chest. Sometimes he would forget a line and have to hold me a while as he thought of it. And then, I had a line which had to be whispered in his ear, so I leaned in close to him, breathing in his warmth and letting my lips brush against his ear. He asked to rehearse that scene several times, and each time we came closer together, his breath became quicker, and his hand, which held mine, squeezed tighter. My cheeks were flushed from excitement as we *pretended* to flirt, our fingers entwined.

And then it happened that we noticed Miss Crawford and Mr. Rushworth going past and we quickly withdrew our hands and continued saying our lines, though we were now stilted and inexpressive. It was then I realized that Henry knew we were going beyond what was appropriate behavior and that he felt as I did in wishing to be more intimate. Once the danger had passed and Mr. Rushworth was gone with Miss Crawford, we stopped and looked at each other acknowledging our narrow escape of discovery and we laughed.

"Shall we continue?" Henry asked me.

It was a loaded question. Now we knew what we were doing and we knew it was unfitting our situation and was very dangerous should we be caught. But his passionate eyes, heavy breath along with my rapid heartbeat and warming body would not let me be rational. All I wanted was another touch.

I coolly replied, "Of course, why ever should we stop? We are very near to perfecting our parts, I believe."

He said, "Oh yes, very close. Perhaps just a little more of the ending scene and we should be the very best Agatha and Frederick that has ever graced the stage."

I smiled knowingly and we began. I moved my chair closer to his as we faced each other so that our knees were nearly touching. He began his lines and reached out for my hand. As he held it, I brought our hands up to my breast so he might feel my heartbeat and that roused him greatly. He leaned closer to me and I recited my lines of affection and then I leaned forward to whisper in his ear. As I did so, he turned his face so that our lips brushed sending a rush of pleasure through my body. I steadied myself by placing my hand on his leg and he assisted my unsteadiness by reaching out to my hold my waist. In this entanglement we held for a moment, our lips so close I could feel his breath, his hand in mine upon my breast he could feel my heart pound. He recovered himself and continued, though his lines were not at all accurate to the book.

"Agatha, I have never felt... you are a superior woman to any I have ever known. I feel that together we might enjoy a felicity unequal to any other couple. Together..."

He pulled me closer so that we were both on the edges of our seats only our entwined hands separating my breast from his chest. I could now feel his quickened heartbeat as well. My hand slid up his leg as his hand lowered from my waist to my upper thigh, his fingers sliding inward.

"Together, we might know blissful delight and I know if you let me in I could teach you to know the heights of elation in..."

I was literally losing my head and was so pressed

against him I felt I could never be close enough, but suddenly we heard a door open and several people came into the room. We quickly separated, taking up our books. The servants were come to the theater to continue working on the stage and curtain. Henry smiled at me and suggested we find a more private place to continue rehearsing. I followed him with all the expectation of allowing him to teach me the heights of elation, only the first door we opened we found Edmund, Miss Crawford and Fanny in the library and we couldn't excuse ourselves away as Fanny greeted us and suggested taking a break for refreshment. The Crawford's were obliged to leave after that but would return after dinner for the full rehearsal that evening so we were forced to wait until hopefully another opportunity that evening.

But another opportunity would not come. Just as we were performing the very scene where our intimacy was earlier heightened and Fredrick held the hand of Agatha to his chest, Julia burst into the room, her face white as a ghost and cried, "My father is come! He is in the hall at this moment!"

Everyone froze in shock and horror! But as I turned to Henry his eyes were still forward and yet, his hand still held mine to his heart. To retain my hand in such a moment was proof of his determination and feelings toward me.

Julia too understood it, and the poor jealous girl turned red as she left in a huff. My brothers and I went directly to greet Father and I learned later that the Crawford's had left. Of course, Father immediately put an end to our theatrical scheme and was very upset, shaming us all. Even Mr. Rushworth felt it and quickly appeased Father by saying he didn't enjoy the idea at all either. But there a hint in his voice of jealousy, for he did not like seeing the connection between Henry and I on the stage.

When Henry returned after two days absence he was completely transformed. I understood why he stayed away, to avoid my father's wrath, but once we were again in the same party he showed no tenderness or feeling towards me at all, only lamenting that the play had been cancelled. He even determined to immediately leave for Bath with some terrible excuse to visit his Uncle! Gone! Just like that all my hopes for him were over!

I was so disappointed and heated that I would talk to no one for days. We dined with Mr. Rushworth and I did not feel like attending to him at all. I could not stand the man's simpering way of talking and constantly eating and self-flattering. I could see that even my father did not warm to him. I received no letters, no contact at all with the Crawford's and I knew I had been used terribly. Now I was so angry, so dissatisfied with all things at Mansfield and so determined NOT to allow Mr. Crawford's behavior to appear to affect me that I resolved the best revenge would be to marry as soon as possible into wealth and freedom that would allow me to travel and quit Mansfield and memories of *him* altogether! So foolish I was! Six months ago my feelings were so temperamental and idiotic I cannot understand how I could have thought that marrying Mr. Rushworth was my escape. It is my prison! My torment! Would that I could go back home to Mansfield! Would that I could have been patient and waited for a letter from the Crawford's. Of course they stayed away, believing my father to be upset with them. They returned soon after I was married and spent many days at Mansfield! Had I ended my engagement and stayed, surely I should have been able to rekindle that affection that seemed so strong from Henry.

And then I received a letter from Mary Crawford that

has completely thrown me into confusion! She hinted that he may be now attached to my cousin Fanny! It is the greatest puzzlement to me! I have obsessed over those two sentences.

"Henry seems to dote on dear Fanny on our daily visits. She is the sweetest of girls and deserves him."

What could that elude to?! He never even looked at or spoke to Fanny in all those weeks he was with us. I cannot believe for the world he would consider Fanny! Not over me! Miss Crawford must mean that Fanny is lucky to have Mr. Crawford as a visiting friend. She must only mean to mention Fanny out of kindness to me. For *she* is nothing to anyone!

Journal Entry
March
Today I saw Mr. Crawford at a party and I was surprised to discover I was still very angry with him. I was as cold to him as I could be. Said nothing and would not meet his eye. I wanted to hear nothing he had to say. I could see he was surprised by my indifference and I am glad of it. I hope he is not unaware that I am mistress of all of Wimpole and Sotherton! *He* could not have provided me such luxury. I made sure he saw me laugh and drink and speak to as many people of consequence as possible. I wanted him to know that I don't think of him at all and I barely consider him an acquaintance. I hope I shall never see him again.

Journal Entry
April
It is the beginning of April and I am all in confusion. Mr. Rushworth is so tedious to listen to and a horror in

the evening, I cannot bear to touch him. His affections are so unwanted. My only consolation is he is leaving for Bath to visit his horrid mother (and unfortunately to bring her back to our house) and I am leaving to visit new yet intimate friends for the Easter holidays in Twickenham. At least there I shall have some entertainment and peace.

Journal Entry
April- Twickenham
I am greatly enjoying my days at Twickenham. Not only do I have lively company with the Aylmers, but Mr. Crawford has visited us. Quite often, in fact, as Henry is staying in Richmond at his uncle's cottage and he appears to be attempting to win back my good opinion. After everything we have been through, I find it difficult to not give in a little to his attentions. I made him color when I mentioned Fanny during one of our walks. I asked him if she had returned any of his affections during his time at Mansfield. He appeared so surprised by it that he actually stopped walking!

He dismissed it, and said there was nothing in it. He said, "I was only showing the natural kindness that would be extended to any member of your family. Perhaps, as Fanny is not used to such attention, she may have perceived it to mean more. But, in fact, there is only one member of the family that I have ever felt close to, that I have shared an affection with before."

Now it was my turn to color. I did not answer him and continued to walk. But he persisted in asking if we were not still friends and I had to eventually answer him that we were. Then he asked if I looked back at our time during Lovers Vows with regret! I could not believe he would bring that up- I was shocked. I did not say another word for several minutes. He waited patiently and I did answer him.

"Our time together was not what I regret."

He smiled and replied, "Nor I. I look at that time fondly and sometimes wonder how things might have been different if we had been allowed to finish the play. I regret that the play was stopped and we all had to part so abruptly. But, now, at least, we may continue our friendship?"

My blushed silence must have spoken my acquiescence for he returned to visit the Aylmers often, and I quite forgot Mr. Rushworth.

We took long walks, getting lost in the twisty old streets of town, talking of nothing, fashions, people, etc. He would exclaim often how pleasant it was to have a friend he could share all his feelings with, someone who would talk with him who was animated and lively. I assumed he was comparing me with sullen, slow Fanny Price who never said a word except to contradict or judge others. I found myself thinking of him all the time when he was gone. Imagining what might have been if my father had not returned and so end our acting schemes. I wondered if there was yet not a way to remedy my error! Could Henry Crawford still love me as he once did? Did he suffer as I did? I had to know!

He visited the next morning, though my friends had planned an outing. I remained behind complaining of a headache and Henry stayed on. I was determined to discover Henry's feelings. I inquired after his sister, Mary, and he assured me that she was still in London. I explained Mr. Rushworth was still in Bath and my sister, Julia, was visiting other relations. She, in fact, was receiving visits from his friend Mr. Yates who had been the originator of our theatre scheme. I also let him know my friends were gone for the entire day and I was quite alone.

He then gave me a look that I knew well and we instantly understood each other. While it was not safe in this home with all the servants about, we determined to go for a ride in his chaise. Only my maidservant was aware of it and in her I had complete trust. We rode to the family home where he was staying and entered to find no one there save a servant who was quickly dismissed. Henry led me through the drawing room to a small library, which was very nicely situated. He chose one of his favorite volumes, explaining he wanted to read a passage to me, and came to sit beside me on the couch. He read a few lines but constantly looked up from the page into my eyes which were constantly upon him. He seemed to hesitate but I placed my hand on his leg, as I had done before, and that served as enough encouragement.

He dropped his book and took hold of me. I gasped with pleasure as he brought his lips to my neck. He whispered,

"And shall we continue our rehearsal? Agatha?"

My entire body quivered with excitement! What a game! I replied, "Oh Fredrick, how I have ached for your return! Will you now teach me the height of elation?"

He pulled me to him and placed his lips on mine! What a kiss! What passion and heat! I was no longer an unpracticed novice and I returned his passion, our tongues tasting each other and my hands exploring his inner thighs. Henry moaned and I knew he was mine. I unbuttoned his trouser fall and pulled up his undershirt. He lay back as I lifted my petticoat and chemise and climbed on top of him. He was in me immediately and I felt such pleasure in moving on top of him that I had not yet known. The warmth and tightness in my belly soon heightened to frenzied ecstasy and all thought left my head as nothing but pleasure and rapture wracked my body. His fingers and lips grasped at everything he could reach. I climaxed until I could take no more and as I slowed he sat up and gently left my body, having no lamb skin protection, covering himself.

But I took him in my hands and he was surprised by my boldness as I was determined to give him the same pleasure I had just experienced.

After, we simply held each other, breathing hard, not wanting to speak or end the moment. But finally, Henry did speak, replaced his trouser fall and begged to be excused. He left and I straightened my petticoat and muslin dress, fixed my hair as best I could without a ladies maid and forced myself to calm so that my color would not be out of turn. After some time, I heard a servant bring some tea into the drawing room and there I waited another ten minutes before Henry returned. He was all smiles and joviality. We soon left the home and he returned me before my friends had arrived. He would not come in, but he promised to call the next day.

I was exhilarated! To know that Henry felt for me as I felt for him! To know that his love had been ever constant. It was my folly in marrying so quickly and not waiting for his return. I must have ruined all his hopes! But now I will make amends. I am determined. I shall leave Mr. Rushworth and elope with Mr. Crawford just as soon as I can procure a divorce. I care nothing for Rushworth's family, nor in fact for the feelings of my father who will surely feel a hit to his sense of pride, though I know he did not even like Rushworth to begin with. My mother will not care at all. I do not care what Julia may think. I cannot continue living in constant fear of intimacy and disgust of my own husband and now I have a secure way to end it! I would have to return to London in a couple days so I had to spend as much time with Henry as possible!

Henry did come the next day to visit and brought with him two friends. They suggested an immediate outing and we drove out into the country where they had organized a lovely picnic. I discovered they were a couple engaged and as they wished to walk alone, Henry and I were left to ourselves, much to our satisfaction.

We walked several minutes into the woods, and finding a rather nice area hidden down a bank at the base of a tree, we grabbed each other and within a minute I was laying in the clovers and he was on top of me, lifting my dress as I unbuttoned his fall. He pushed into me and I cried out in pleasure knowing no one was within distance to hear. He had brought protection so we could fully enjoy each other as long as we wanted. As we laid together, we observed how little time we had left together here and wouldn't it be wonderful if we somehow had more time. Driving back, I suspected the other couple might have had as enjoyable a 'walk' as we.

This evening over cards, Henry and I flirted openly, for who would care here, and when we had a chance, we escaped the room and found a hidden closet which felt like our moments hiding behind the theater curtain, only this time we fulfilled our every desire and I found I greatly enjoyed being pushed into a wall from behind, his hands on my breasts, mouth on my neck and body pressed up into me. I could not get enough of him!

Before we left each other this evening, I invited him to visit me in London, telling him I must have him again.

Journal Entry

May

So much has happened, I hardy know where to begin! Back in London it was several days before I saw Mr. Crawford again. Mr. Rushworth and his mother had returned from Bath. His friend, Mr. Harding, was visiting and I had had no chance at all to be alone or even venture outdoors. All that time I fantasized about Mr. Crawford, reliving every moment. Finally, I did seize a chance and was able to leave my house on Wimpole Street to go shopping for some new ribbon. I dismissed my maidservant and she happily left on her own errands. I walked all the way to the home where he would be staying and left my card for his sister, Miss Crawford. Lingering on the pavement near the house for a full ten minutes I began to lose hope that he was home. I became frightened that our week away together was only fun to him and now that we were back he would refuse to see me! And then, there he was standing in the doorway. Henry had seen the message and walked out to meet me.

At first, he seemed nervous about me coming to his Uncle's home but I convinced him that no one was watching me or suspecting anything. Then I whispered a few things that I had fantasized about while we were apart. Now he did not seem in the least like he had any reservations and he took me through the gated, cobblestoned carriage passage around the side of the house and a large, covered coach stood in the narrow passage. He opened the door of the coach and stood like a footman with a big grin on his face. I excitedly jumped in, sat on the cushioned seat, and he clicked the door shut behind us. We wasted no time and we were now experts of engaging each other with removing as little clothing as possible. He leaned back on the seat and I climbed on top of him as he kissed me all over. God, it was good to feel him again. A relief after several days away, not knowing for sure if it would be continued.

While in the midst of our passion I spoke to him about running away together. He seemed quite surprised but I assured him it was the only way, for if we were to continue to be together my husband would surely discover us. That seemed to excite him, so I spoke more of 'my husband' and told him how bad we were being several times until he agreed running away was what we must do. Now I knew Henry's game. He loved to be bad, and so I made sure we were very bad together. We were very bad in my husband's coach and we were very bad in the gardens. We were very bad in his uncle's house and the most exciting of all, we were very bad late at night, in my own bedchamber, with Mr. Rushworth snoozing only a couple doors away. My maidservant was the only one who knew and she ensured Henry was able to escape Wimpole unnoticed.

Eventually, Mr. Rushworth seemed to have heard something of my meeting with him in Twickenham, and then that I had been seen with him again here in London. I, of course, laughed it off as casual acquaintances with mutual friends greeting each other. I felt that his observant friend, Mr. Harding, was the one placing doubt into Mr. Rushworth's ears and things became so difficult at home that I could not move from room to room without feeling scrutinized. I was finally able to escape when we had gone out to a luncheon and I made excuses of feeling ill. Mr. Rushworth was obliged to stay so I had my chance to see Henry.

I found him in the stables behind his house and he was a vision, bare chested, brushing down a tawny mare, wearing his breeches and riding boots. He was surprised when I crept up behind him ran my fingers down his back! He quickly pulled me into the paddock and whispered rather harshly that I was taking very risky chances. But after a moment of me rubbing and kissing his chest, he relented and we were soon hidden behind stacked bales of hay in a romp which involved his head under my chemise.

As he helped remove blades of hay from my hair, I told him how my husband was becoming suspicious and that his nosy friend was inferring. Henry did seem concerned and we decided to make our escape immediately or be discovered. Mr. Rushworth came home shortly after I had returned and I maintained that I was ill and stayed in bed. He suggested calling the doctor, but I convinced him to wait until the morning. That evening I swore my maidservant to secrecy and we packed as much as I could carry in my bags. After the house was asleep, I walked out alone into the night and Henry's carriage was there.

We set off and he drove nearly all night. We stopped at an inn to rest and the horses needed rest as well. I couldn't sleep but Henry assured me that we would not be discovered. There was something in his tone that seemed strange to me. Instead of an exciting first night together, he slept soundly until morning. The first days were fine as we travelled to different places, I made sure to pleasure him every time we stopped, and he seemed to be enjoying our adventure, but then he began to be agitated and nervous. After drinking one evening, he inexplicably brought up Fanny! He said that he missed her gentle smiles and soft ways, and that now he had become the man she accused him of being!

He was restless and anxious and would not let me console him. He went on and on about how he had begun to have real, tender feelings for Fanny and she would not accept him because she knew what he really was. He said he had tried to show Fanny she was wrong, but now, now, he was infinitely worse then she would ever have thought him to be. He lamented losing her friendship forever knowing he would never be allowed to see her again.

I screamed at him that if he had loved Fanny why then would he give his attentions to me? I reminded him that he did not truly love Fanny, it was I who excited his passions! He would not even look at me. I stormed away to the bedroom and cried myself to sleep, hoping that in the morning he would be sober and realize that it was me he loved and I would love him despite his errors in moral judgement, for they were only errors in his desire and love for me! How could love be immoral?

When he was feeling less troubled I explained that I loved him for everything he was, not some ridiculous level of piety held by Fanny Price's standards. I knew him. I loved him. And that seemed to hold him for a while. But as the days worn on, he became agitated again, speaking of his sister, "This might affect her accepting your brother Edmund. This could sever all acquaintance with your family!"

I replied, "I thought your sister never intended to accept him because she would not marry a clergyman."

He went on, lamenting, "This might affect Mrs. Grant (his sister) who lives as such close neighbors to Mansfield Park! I shall never be in any of their society again!"

I yelled that he had gone too far, that he was making too much of this. "Once we are married everything will be as it was before between all of us."

But he would not hear of it or listen to reason! He would not touch me now and all he did was complain about losing Fanny. Fanny this and Fanny that! I thought I should like to kill Fanny. But then I realized that it was not Fanny at fault. That perhaps he had really loved her and that I had simply been a sensual allurement and a distraction. Perhaps I had really ruined his chances for a felicitous home. But what did I care? If he did not marry me, then I am ruined. I will have lost everything! Am I not the one that sacrificed everything? Honor, reputation, family, home, comfort, fortune?

We fought and I stayed with the continued hope of his marrying me in the end after remorse and regret had run its course. But he did not. I accused him of seducing me away from my husband and demanded to understand why he had run away with me if he never intended to marry? He accused me of showing no reserve or caution when I came to see him. He said my reckless public behavior forced him to flee with me.

I hate him for what he has done to me. I hate myself for what I have done to us both. With no hope of marriage, I finally left him with nowhere to go. I sent word to my father that I was returning and he has sent me to stay in shameful isolation, never to be allowed back at Mansfield Park.

I am undone. I could not be more wretched. Curse foul, lying, deceitful men!

LOUISA'S FALL
Persuasion

Louisa Musgrove's Diary,
October Entry

I'm falling. Absolutely falling for Captain Fredrick Wentworth. Wentworth had come to visit his sister who is the new tenant of Kellynch, the neighboring Elliot family home of my brother's wife, Mary. It all sounds very involved and tiresome but Captain Wentworth made our acquaintance at a party and he was the most handsome man I had ever seen! Tall, broad shoulders, dark hair, clean shaved. He wore a captain's uniform when I first saw him at dinner and I could not keep my eyes off of him! My younger sister stood there with her mouth hanging open, for her best experience in seeing men was our near neighbor, Charles Hayter, who was quite plain in comparison. Captain Wentworth was everything perfect in a man. He had manners, looks, experience (he had fought in the war!) and fortune.

Since I was just returned from completing school at Exeter, and he was returned from his many adventures on his ship, there was much to talk about. He was so kind! And lively! Not some tiresome old dullard reciting reports of naval undertakings, but an adventurous storyteller who conveyed the names and actions and feelings of real people in real peril. His stories were so exciting and I loved hearing him speak. His voice is like dripping honey. He is so smart too. Half the words he uses I have no idea about, but I am simply captivated by him.

He has come often to see us at Uppercross, several times now, and he is a spirited dancer. Luckily, Anne Elliot was staying with us and she could play the pianoforte so well, (much better than me and I would rather dance anyways) that we were able to dance quite a lot. I rather felt for Anne as she never dances and she has quite given herself up for an old maid, otherwise, why would she not wish to dance with Captain Wentworth? Anyone would! But all the better for me.

I longed to be alone with him, hoping we might be able to speak more openly with each other. Finally, we were all gone on a long walk through the country together, the six of us, including my sister, brother, his wife and Anne. But as the path narrowed, I ensured that I was right next to the Captain and I spoke as much as possible of my own constancy, devotion and steadfastness, which he honored me for! I directed our walk to Winthrop, where our party separated. I made sure that my sister, Henrietta, split our party to call on Charles Hayter, who hoped to marry her. I had to get Henrietta out of the way, as she was becoming exasperating with her flirtations towards Captain Wentworth. With Mary and Anne too fatigued to do anything but sit and wait for them, I led the Captain into the hedgerows and continued talking of my firmness of decisions and easily told him of my sister's nearly changing her mind not to go to Winthrop to visit with Mr. Hayter. He then spoke with real feeling, giving all the encouragement in the world. He pulled down a hazel nut and spoke of its strength to have still survived and he compared its strength and firmness to me! Then he called me beautiful and happy and complemented my powers of mind! I was stunned and I am sure my face blushed, for I became quite warm. How easy it would have been for him to propose at that moment. But he did not. I was not dismayed however, and continued to ensure he knew my character. I made certain he knew I detested the Elliot pride, displayed by my horrible sister-in-law Mary. Anne was loved, but then, she was the quiet obliging type. My brother wanted to marry her first and it is too bad she refused him.

Wentworth seemed surprised that Anne would refuse him. And I understand, I mean, looking at Anne, what better prospects could she really have? But no matter. Once my brother and sister returned from Winthrop, Charles Hayter was with them and it appeared my plan worked. Henrietta was once again attached to Hayter and she was out of the picture. I had Wentworth all to myself.

We walked together, just the two of us in the front, all the way back to Uppercross, stopping only once to allow frail Anne to get a ride home on a gig with Wentworth's sister. We spoke of many things, and he gave me many hints of his attachment to me. He moved hanging nettles in the hedges out of my way and warned me of a fallen limb on the path. So kind! So attentive! I was certain that once we got home, he would propose. But he did not. I must devise another way for us to be alone together.

November Entry

We are in Lyme! A wonderful scheme! It all happened so quickly! Before our trip together, Captain Wentworth went away for a couple of days, and the entire time I fretted and agonized about whether he would ever return. I wondered if I had done or said something wrong that had driven him off. But he returned only from visiting a friend, Captain Harville in Lyme. He mentioned enjoying it and wanting to go back, so I insisted we should all go together until the entire plan was made! Charles and Mary, Henrietta, Anne, Captain Wentworth and I were to all go! I knew Wentworth would approve of my insisting I had my own way. I was not to be put off or easily persuaded. I was the one who convinced my parents to allow us to go now, instead of waiting till Summer. I think my mother knew that this trip would ensure my engagement.

Arriving in Lyme, we had a marvelous dinner and secured our rooms. We all walked down to the seashore, where the breezy salt air filled my lungs. Looking out on the sea, I could not help but think that I should always like to live near it, its beauty was so captivating. I felt such a sense of hope that the sea would soon become an important part of my life. We walked out onto the harbor, called the Cobb, and Captain Wentworth introduced us to some of his friends, Captain and Mrs. Harville, and a Captain Benwick. It was an honor to meet them and I did my best to make him feel that I would be perfectly placed among the party. I fawned over every little thing in the Harville's tiny house and praised the Navy extensively, knowing this would please Wentworth. I wondered at Captain Benwick, so secluded in his little corner with his shelves of books, the poor man suffering over the loss of his fiancé some months earlier. To have finally come into his fortune only to lose his waiting betrothed was heartbreaking. And now he lived with his late fiancé's brother, Captain Harville. How strange. And how sad that the poor girl waited all that time to be married, only to die just before it might take place! I determined I would never allow a long engagement, which would be unbearable. Already, waiting for a proposal was intolerable. I hoped soon to show Wentworth my determination and fortitude that he so highly prizes, then get him alone so he may propose.

We returned to the inn to dress for dinner. I shared a room with Anne and Henrietta and, as we were not far down the hall from Wentworth, I fantasized about meeting him in the hall by his door, coming upon him. With a sly look, I would follow him in, where we could be alone and he would instantly grab me, passionately tell me of his enduring love, and propose, whereby I would breathlessly answer yes and he would kiss me, holding me in his strong arms.

But alas, though I dressed faster than the other women and went alone into the hallway, even lingering outside his door, I was too late. He had already gone down and was joined by Charles. Then his friends joined us and we listened to Wentworth and Harville regale us with stories of adventures on the sea. I noticed several times that Anne and Captain Benwick seemed deep in conversation, and I wondered what he may be talking to her about. He seemed very passionate about whatever his subject was and I became quite curious as to the sudden intimacy he seemed to share with Anne, though they had just met! Not even Wentworth and I had had such intimate whispering conversations that would rouse such fervor.

That evening, as we all went up to our rooms, I

delayed for a moment on the stairs to be the last following Wentworth. Henrietta and Anne were already gone to bed and he was just above me on the stairs. We were alone. He proceeded up and I quickly followed after him. I paused when he stopped to open his door. He turned surprised, and I blushed with a bow, saying, 'Excuse me, sir'. He bowed. This was his chance. His chance to invite me in, to have me alone in his room, to propose, to do anything! I was completely disposed to be at his command. But he only said, "Good night." And was gone!

I stood outside his room for a moment. I thought about knocking, but that would be completely improper and might damage his view of me. I walked slowly down the hall hoping he would suddenly call me back. But he did not.

My disappointment is so great, I cannot sleep! Why would he not take that opportunity? Does he have something else planned? Now dear diary, I tell you I am more determined than ever. Tomorrow I shall be always near him. I shall be playful, determined and witty. He will love me by the end of tomorrow and I am sure all will be settled before going home to Uppercross. I have every hope!

December Entry

I am well. I am well. I may now write when several weeks ago I may have been dead. I had fallen. The very next day after my last entry we had all gone for a walk by the sea. I foolishly jumped off the narrow stone stairs of the Cobb, expecting Captain Wentworth to catch me. But he did not. I had become unconscious and remained that way for some time. I do not remember any of it. They told me I sometimes awoke, but I have no memory of falling, or being brought to the home of Captain Harville, or being attended by the surgeon. My first memories are of Mrs. Harville softly singing to me and when I awoke she was so gentle. Over the days, I grew stronger under her care, although I dreaded my shrill sister-in-law Mary entering my room. I often pretended to sleep when she would come so that I would not have to hear her go on and on about everything and everyone. What was only annoying before, now became a torment. But Mrs. Harville kept her away as much as possible and my cloudy thoughts eventually cleared, though my body was still weak, and I wondered why I had not seen Captain Wentworth. It was days before I ventured to ask such a question. Mrs. Harville explained how he had taken Anne and Henrietta back home to break the news of my condition to my parents, and how he had returned and stayed until he knew I was no longer in great danger. But then he left and has not been back again. I know in my heart that he has given me up. No man who truly loved would ever leave the side of his love while she was ailing. He would have stayed, been by my side. He would not have left me, if he had loved me. That is why he did not propose. No, Wentworth did not love me. I thought it over and over and cried bitterly and could not eat. But Mrs. Harville talked with me, encouraged me, and showed me that I have much to be thankful for.

I survived and have been very well cared for. Better than I could have ever imagined. Captain Benwick gave up his own room to me, I have come to understand. I am still weak and must lie in this bed, but I am growing stronger, in body and mind. I was idiotic, headstrong, and persuaded into thinking I was in love, persuaded into thinking I would attract him by showing a fortitude of mind when, in fact, I was being obstinate and reckless. Ours had not been a relationship based on love, but only flirtation, lively conversation. I was silly. I blush thinking of it.

How I behaved is humiliating to me now. Demanding we all come to visit here on a whim and ordering everyone about, to go for a walk, and go to the shops, and go to the Cobb. To make him jump me down the steps to the lower Cobb, acting absolutely ridiculous, like a school girl! Only wanting him to touch me, only wanting him to catch me around the waist so I would feel that momentary exhilaration of his hands on me. I showed no maturity of mind or spirit! I refused to listen to him as he warned me against jumping again. I fell by my own blunder, I fell by my own impatience. I have fallen, from dignity, from honor. He must think I'm a simpleton. But he was encouraging and he did speak such things as to make me believe he was attached to me! But he is gone now, and I am left to my caretakers and my own regretful thoughts.

My brother and Mary are gone now at least, so I may have some peace. That sister-in-law Mary is so tedious with her constant complaints! Her shrill voice sends tremors through me and even my brother is no comfort, as he does not know what to say to me other than to talk of the weather and where Mary will go shopping that day. At least they are gone and Mrs. Harville has her home back. I feel for Mrs. Harville who waits on me day and night, seemingly tireless, but I see the darkness under her eyes. I endeavored to sit up to show her my strength and that she need not be with me at all times. Captain Benwick is often standing in the door, offering his assistance or bringing me food and drink. I wished he would not stand there. I did not want to be looked at. I must look appalling, my hair a tangled nest, my pallid skin and dull gaze. He sometimes comes in to retrieve a book or something from his room and always asks if there is anything he can do for my comfort. I jokingly asked for a dresser and not twenty minutes later, a young maid appeared who spend an hour washing, brushing and styling my hair. I knew it was all Captain Benwick's doing because Mrs. Harville was quite surprised to see my hair up in rings.

One afternoon, Captain Benwick offered to read to me, to give Mrs. Harville a break, and assured her that it was nothing improper as the house maid would be our chaperone. He sat and read poetry to me and at first I felt it was tiresome and didn't listen, but then I found that I enjoyed the change of company and his soft voice. He read some poetry that was somber, reflected lost time and lost hearts and suffering evermore, and I cried, feeling its application to myself. I wished he would leave and take his mourning spirit with him. He immediately put down the volume and tried to find something more cheerful to read to me. He read a story, apparently suggested to him by Anne Elliot, which was full of recovery, fortitude and regaining inner strength. I felt we both had lessons to take from such texts.

The next day he did the same, and Mrs. Harville went away for a couple hours. He stayed with me the entire time, sending the maid away to fetch tea or food. He read to me Scott's Marmion and The Lady of the Lake. After a few days, he told the maid she could continue about her house work and that the door would remain open and it was not improper as he was considered my caretaker after all. I looked forward to his coming every day, for his voice was very pleasant, his company soothing, and though I didn't fully listen to half the things he read to me, descriptions of birds and trees from Wordsworth or images of the spring from Blake, it mattered not what he read, it was just him being in the room with me that made it a comfort.

After a fortnight of him sitting with me nearly every day, he came during an evening. It had become frigid cold outside, and somehow my fire had gone out. I was so cold I feared I might become ill. I called out and it was Benwick who came to my door so fast! He quickly put more blankets on me, gave me a shawl, and tended the fire. Once the fire was going, he woke the maid and had her go make hot tea.

When she was gone, I still shivered and he pulled my bed closer to the fire (how strong he was, as it was a large bed- his own bed in fact- that I was lying in). I was shivering and he felt my hand. "Oh, how cold your hand is!" He kneeled and took my hands in his. His hands were so warm, I do not remember anything feeling so wonderful. He held my hands in his by the fire and I began to warm. Not just from the fire, and not just from his hands, for I felt a warmth in my belly, and as I looked up at his face (he was turned away looking at the fire), I felt my face blush, thinking he was not unhandsome and I was surprised I did not discern it before. He glanced at me, saw that I was looking at him, and then held my gaze.

The maid's footsteps were heard returning and he let go of my hands and stood up quickly. He said a quick goodnight, thanked the maid and left. I held the teacup, but it did not give the warmth and comfort of Captain Benwick's hands.

The next day his countenance had changed. He approached uncertain and stood in the doorway, but a smile from me encouraged him to sit with me, and he pulled from his shelf Lord Byron. The change in his selection, I believe, arose from his brightened spirits, which only a touch and a gaze in the firelight can engender. Like any woman who is read poetry by a man, I felt the words had been written expressly for me. I rewrite the beginning of the poem here, so that I may reread it over and over.

She walks in beauty, like the night
Of cloudless climes and starry skies;
And all that's best of dark and bright
Meet in her aspect and her eyes.

January Entry

Benwick is with me every day now. When before I would wish him away, now I beg him to stay. His low, velvety voice is soothing to my aching head, and his words rouse me. He came sometimes in the evening, after the house had quieted, choosing poetry that sounds much better read in a hushed voice in the light of a crackling fire. He read a poem by Buonarroti, this one so romantic, I reached out for him, and he willingly took my hand. He read the last lines again, this time by heart, looking right at me, and I knew he was not simply reading the lines, he was declaring them to me!

Love takes me captive; beauty binds my soul;
Pity and mercy with their gentle eyes
Wake in my heart a hope that cannot cheat.
What law, what destiny, what fell control,
What cruelty, or late or soon, denies
That death should spare perfection so complete?

I could not meet his eyes, but I could not stop smiling. Over the course of the week, he read many other stories to me, many involving life on the sea. Adventures of naval captains in war and facing down storms. I began to learn the naval terms and dream about the exotic places they visit. One evening, I told Benwick that I wanted to hear more of the romantic poetry. Benwick obliged and held my hand, which was now regular whenever we were alone. He began to read Keats' Bright Star and after the first stanza I squeezed his hand gently. He looked surprised but gratified, and he squeezed back. As he continued reading, I ran my fingers through his. He caught his breath but did not retreat.

Reaching the last lines, he moved forward, almost whispering them to me.

Pillow'd upon my fair love's ripening breast,
To feel for ever its soft fall and swell,
Awake forever in a sweet unrest,
Still, still to hear her tender-taken breath,
And so live ever or else swoon to death.

I was taken by his words so cloaked in messages to me. I longed to pull him to my breast, so that he might feel my racing heart. Our fingers entwined, the fire crackling, and the only sound, our slow breaths and my heart drumming in my ears. His eyes flickered like firelight upon mine and I felt a rush, a rush that I had never known before. A tightness in in my chest, a dizziness, a blush, a tingle deep in my body, a loss of all thought. I leaned forward to him and he leaned forward to me. He whispered my name, "Miss Musgrove." As our lips came close to touching, I whispered back, "Captain Benwick." I closed my eyes, waiting for the longed-for kiss. I could feel his breath upon my lips. But the kiss did not come!

I opened my eyes and he had retreated. He gently let go of my hands. I must have looked devastated, for he rapidly (and hardly intelligibly) told me that I was a most exquisite creature, and that he did not want to dishonor me by being too forward, and he felt all that was tender towards me. But in his eyes, I saw pain. As he turned, I saw him glance at a drawer in the table by his bed, and then he departed.

After a few moments of recovery, I opened the drawer to find a small locket. Within was a tiny braid of hair. This must have belonged to his late fiancé, so recently lost, not five months ago. Now I understood him. He felt guilty, guilty about his feelings for me. How could a man who claimed to have loved with such devotion, who mourned every moment of every day, suddenly now develop an affection for another?

While it pained me to think that he was suffering, and I worried that he would not come again to see me, I was, in my heart, soaring. His own reluctance showed his true attachment to me. His self-reproach showed a steadfastness that honored his lost love and a conscience that honored him.

I have always been high-spirited, more inclined to talk than read, dance than study music. I have never sat this still for so long in all my life. I have never had such periods of quiet solitude and reflection, with only my thoughts as a companion. Captain Benwick has shown me another world of feeling and experience. Through his readings and words and warmth he has shown me real passion, and in return I have felt it!

Too long I had fretted over Wentworth and whether he would return. I had let his absence define whether I should succumb to injury or strive to endure. He does not love me. I never loved him. Vanity, social rank, and foolishness had anchored me to him. I had been playing a game for which I did not understand the rules or even what I was trying to win. Even if he came back now, I would not receive his hand, no matter what expectation was on me. He abandoned me, and no man in love would ever have left the side of the woman he loves with no just reason. No longer will I be boisterous or unruly as I was. No longer will I fret or shake as I have. I shall now be content to read poetry by the firelight with Captain Benwick, his fingers entwined with mine. I shall show him that my love, my steady, passionate, resolute love, can be the cure to his anguish.

I left the locket on the table top, and when the next evening he came, for he stayed away all day, he knelt by my side as soon as Mrs. Harville quitted the room. The maid quickly left as well, for she knew we wanted to be alone. He apologized for his abrupt parting last evening and begged that he might be able to read to me again. Then he saw the locket. The evident pain on his face showed that I was right in his feelings of guilt and possibly even betrayal. I asked about her. I told him she must have been a superior woman. And he began to talk of her in such terms as would shame the romantic poets. He spoke of losing her as like the blue sky turning gray, yet never raining, like his heart had been smothered, choked, and all love was sunk deep into the dark well of his grief.

It did pain me to hear him speak of her, and a strange jealousy rose in me, jealousy of a dead woman. I wondered how I might ever take her place in his heart.

I told him, "You have much love in your heart."

Then as if reading my thoughts, he said, "Though she will always be in my heart, I know that I cannot hold back that love which might rise in me again. And you, you alone, have begun to clear the skies for me."

We sat in silence, listening to the crackle of the fire. I reached out my hand and his fingers slid through mine.

I said, "I just want you here. Close to me."

He bent and kissed my hand and I embraced him and laid his head against my breast. He must have heard my heart thundering in his ear. At long last, he sat up. We faced each other, our hands touching. I wasn't going to let him leave the room this time without more.

"Captain," I whispered. I let go with one of my hands and slid my fingers up his arm to hold him. I ran my other fingers up to his cheek and he closed his eyes, his breath becoming shallow. His long curls had fallen over his eyes and I reached up to push them back. I had longed to run my fingers through his mess of curly hair, and as my fingers ran through, I touched his ear which made him open his eyes wide and gasp. I sat up straighter and tightened my hold of him.

I did not know what to say, so I began to recite Elizabeth Browning. A poem that I had recently read so often, I knew now by heart.

"And wilt thou have me fashion into speech
the love I bear thee, finding words enough,
and hold the torch out, while the winds are rough,
between our faces, to cast light on each?"

His eyes shone and I moved closer to him. His hands reached out and held me around the waist. He continued,

"I drop it at thy feet. I cannot teach
my hand to hold my spirit so far off
from myself- me- that I should bring thee proof
in words, of love hid in me, out of reach."

He pulled me closer and my hands were now both in his hair. I continued, whispering,

"Nay, let the silence of my womanhood
Commend my woman-love to thy belief,
Seeing that I stand un-won, however wooed."

He brought me up then, to where I was near sitting on his lap. I brought my hands down to his upper arms to hold on to him, feeling his tensing strength. His lips were so close to mine that I had had no doubt of his intentions to follow through this time. He said,

"And rend the garment of my life, in brief,
by a most dauntless, voiceless fortitude,
lest one touch of this heart convey its grief."

He looked at me in silence for a moment, and then kissed me, with a passion I never imagined possible. Our bodies came together and he held me close, kissing me over and over until the pale orange of dawn peeked above the horizon. He left me then, but promised to return after I had rested and had breakfast. How could I have deserved such happiness! To have found a true passionate love and a real hope for a felicitous life, when not six weeks ago I thought that I would not live.

I slept a few hours, and after a small breakfast and a chat with Mrs. Harville, who remarked that I was looking rather well, I told her I wanted to stand and perhaps sit by the window. She assisted me at first, as I felt weak for the lack of moving for so long. But once on my feet, I felt stronger and slowly walked to the seat by the window. Mrs. Harville added extra cushions to the seat and I looked out on the ocean view. Opening the window slightly, I breathed in the salty air and said aloud that I longed to walk again by the water's edge.

"And so you shall!" Captain Benwick had returned, smiling broadly. He sat with me and we talked about the weather until Mrs. Harville left. He took my hand and kissed it, explaining how he had to go away for the day, but that he hoped to visit me again this evening. I told him I looked forward to feeling his hands in mine again. I asked him to help me walk and he slowly lifted me, his hands on my waist. I felt a shudder of excitement. With one of his arms wrapped around me and the other holding my hand, we walked up and down the room several times until I was too tired to continue. He lowered me back down on his bed and sat beside me.

"You shall soon be strong enough to venture outdoors again. I am amazed by your determination."

I said, "Thank you, Captain Benwick. It is you that brings me this liveliness. It is for your visit tonight that I wish to have strength."

He stared at me a moment, and looking at the door to ensure no one was there, he leaned down and kissed me deeply. He swore to return once the maid had gone to bed.

I slept most of the afternoon and insisted that I eat in the seat by the window for supper. Mrs. Harville even assisted me in walking around the room a little, and with every step I felt strength returning to my legs. I asked to have my hair brushed and pinned up and changed into my cotton chemise nightgown with the lace.

That evening, I listened as the house went quiet, and every sound in the house made me look to the door in expectation. I must have fallen asleep, for I awoke to see Benwick silhouetted as he tended the fire. He had removed his top coat and jacket, wearing only a waistcoat over his white linen shirt.

I sat up and tried to smooth my hair and untangle my blankets before calling to him. He rushed over when he saw that I was awake and sat by me, his hands instantly in mine.

"I am sorry to be so late, Miss Musgrove. If you are not too tired, I have something for you. I left this morning to retrieve it, for I wanted your approval."

I wondered what it could possibly be as he fumbled with his waistcoat pockets. He held out a small box. My eyes widened as he opened it, revealing a topaz jeweled gold ring.

"It was my mother's before she passed, and it was my grandmother's on my father's side before that. If you approve of it, I would like for you to have it, to wear when we are wed... if you will accept me." He took my hands again in his and repeated fervently, "Of course, if you'll accept me."

I was in such amazement by the moment that I did not immediately speak, while his eyes pleaded for an answer.

I replied with Browning's words, for I had none of my own,

"Love me for love's sake, that evermore thou mayst love on, through love's eternity."

His eyes shone in the firelight as he placed the ring on my finger to try it on. I said, "It is perfect."

And he whispered, "Miss Musgrove."

I smiled and said, "Please, Captain, call me Louisa."

His mouth parted in surprise and he replied, "And then you must call me James."

I leaned forward, inviting a kiss, and as his lips brushed mine, I whispered. "James." It was so strange and sensual to call a man by his name. He kissed me and his name repeated over and over in my head. My body trembled as he wrapped an arm around my waist and pulled me closer to him. Perhaps it was the blanket that fell to the side revealing my legs below the knee, or his realization that I wore only my chemise (I had always worn a robe to bed before), but he placed his hand in my hair and pulled me to him for a kiss that made my whole body shake. I tasted his tongue and I wasn't thinking about being proper, I was only thinking of being as close to Benwick as I could.

He kissed my neck and ran his fingers over the short lace sleeves of my nightgown, pushing them down around my shoulders. My hands were in his hair as he kissed my shoulders and then my chest. I whispered his name, "Oh, James," which encouraged him to continue. As he pulled gently at the front satin strings to loosen the chemise, his other hand slowly raised up my waist, where he gently lifted and kissed my breasts, sending waves of pleasure through my body. I felt a deep tingle and soft ache within me and I arched my body upwards to sit in his lap.

I felt him, through his thin trousers, aroused between my legs. He moaned and held me tighter, his tongue caressing my breasts. He looked up at me and my tongue touched his, bringing him back up into a full embrace, kissing my lips, moving our hips softly together. The only layer between us was his trouser fall, which could so easily be unbuttoned.

He said, "My dear, Louisa, we must marry as soon as we may. For how will I resist you, every night, staying here in my own bed."

I began to unbutton him. His tongue was once again in my mouth. I felt neither tired or weak. I just wanted him. I knew that we must wait to fully consummate our marriage, but I was curious and wanted to feel him.

"Louisa!" His whispered cry was more desirous than a

plea to stop, so I pulled back the trouser fall and felt him between my legs. We both gasped as our skin touched and I placed my hands on him. His fingers in turn reached under my chemise, and with his touch on my breasts, and then across my belly and down between my legs, I felt that I could not get a breath! I moved to crouch over him as we caressed each other, my need to feel him inside me was so strong that I began to lower myself over him. He slowly took my hands back in his and he lifted my arms. I thought he was going to pull off my chemise, but he kissed my lips sweetly and said that we must stop, as I was a maid, he must honor me.

We held each other breathing hard for a moment, but he kissed me again and I ran my tongue over his lips hungrily. I felt such desire that I lifted his shirt, leaned down and ran my tongue down his chest. I opened his trouser fall further to bring him into my mouth. His breathing became rapid, and then I felt his fingers reach beneath my chemise and slide inside me. Such pleasure I had never known and it wracked my body! I rolled my tongue and lips over him and he pressed his fingers into me until finally we reached the point of absolute rapture! Lifting my chin, he pulled away. He turned, and I straightened my chemise, trying to catch my breath. He had buttoned his trousers and stood, lit by the glowing embers in the fireplace. He kissed me several more times, straightened my blankets, and held my hands tightly. Finally, I gave him back the ring to keep safe until the wedding.

"My Louisa, I shall speak to Captain Harville in the morning, as I will no longer be able to hide my adoration and regard for you. You are my blue sky, dear Louisa. I wish never to be parted from you again."

He left the room and I laid awake for a while, still feeling the tinges of pleasure from his fingers.

The next morning, Captain Benwick returned with his friend Captain Harville by his side. Captain Harville smiled at me, but looked distraught in his eyes. He called to his wife to come speak with him and Captain Benwick kneeled by my side.

He said to the effect of, "I have spoken to Harville and told him of my intentions towards you. He was surprised, as I am sure everyone will be. He approves, but I know how he must be feeling in regard to his poor sister."

James looked down for a moment to recover himself. I understood that only time would remove his grief, but our love will be stronger for our losses.

He carefully lifted me out of bed and moved me to the seat by the window. He quietly repeated his desire to marry as quickly as we could, and I promised him I would be strong enough to walk unassisted by the time wedding arrangements could be made. I knew we would not be as free to be left alone now as before, when there had been no suspicion of a connection between us, but as long as we could steal kisses now and then, I could wait for marriage for our next night together. We smiled at each other for several minutes, wishing to kiss but not daring while the Harvilles stood not far out of the door. They soon returned and congratulations filled the room.

Benwick left, for he had to write to my father. Once all is settled, he said he must also write to Captain Wentworth, who I am certain will be not be saddened by my change of heart.

JANE'S INDULGENCE
Emma

Dear Diary,
Summer in Weymouth

I have been terribly neglectful of writing since my arrival in Weymouth. The Campbells and I have been so busy with social calls, outings and parties that I simply drop into bed each night too tired to write anything. We have been to several private family parties and my dearest friend, basically a sister, Miss Campbell, had spent most of her time trying very hard not to look at a young man named Mr. Dixon. He is rich and agreeable and lives in Ireland. He described his home in Baly-craig so beautifully, showing us the lovely drawings he had done himself, that Miss Campbell and I couldn't help expressing our wish to see it one day.

And then he was always there. In every social circle we found ourselves in, Mr. Dixon was there, and Miss

Campbell showed no restraint in her delight. He was soon courting her and would often come to hear each of us play and sing, read to each other, and compare our drawings. I would chaperone them on lovely long walks, of course having to stay back to rest just long enough for them to have some time alone as I thought they would enjoy. And as I watched them fall in love, I could not help feeling sadness for myself. For what were all my accomplishments in art and music and education if I could not be happy in love.

I have no inheritance, no family connections. My mother and father died long ago, and after spending my childhood in Highbury with my Aunt Bates, I came to live with Colonel Campbell, a friend of my father's, when I was nine. So I have been brought up with the benefit of the London Masters, yet I am expected to be a governess. For what man of any fortune would marry me? I have often seen men look at me with interest, but then my circumstances are discovered, and I am no longer of any consequence. Soon I am approaching one and twenty, and cannot impose on the Campbells any longer. I must complete the sacrifice, retire from all the pleasures of life, of rational intercourse, equal society, peace, and hope, to penance and mortification forever, to be a teacher.

*　　　　　　*　　　　　　*

A New Acquaintance

We have made a new acquaintance this evening at a small party at the Dixon's. A man from Enscombe in Yorkshire by the name of Frank Churchill. He apparently entered the room while I was singing at the pianoforte. Miss Campbell told me he simply stood in the doorway watching me without speaking to anyone, and when he did, it was to enquire about becoming acquainted with me! We were introduced and though I did not speak much, for I couldn't think of a single interesting thing to say, he was quite lively, and I learned that though he was raised by his uncle in Enscombe, his father, Mr. Weston, lived in Highbury! Miss Campbell quickly pointed out that I grew up there with my aunt and grandmother before coming to live with Campbells. Mr. Churchill was amazed, claimed to know of the Bates, and wanted to hear all about it. I tried to speak of my childhood, but much of it was very dull and as my Aunt Bates enjoys speaking so much, I had become accustomed to remaining quite silent most of the time. But we did talk about the beautiful country there and how lovely it would be to visit with family again. Later, he asked that I play again, and when I tried to protest that my voice was tired, he said that he would sing. So, with the Dixon's and Mrs. Campbell's permission, I came to play for Mr. Frank Churchill. I played, and he stood beside me at the piano, singing with a clear, strong voice that surprised me in its elegance.

As I lay here in bed, I am struck with how much I am thinking of him. He really did have lovely eyes. They simply sparkled as he talked. He was so animated! A man like that, so handsome, so wealthy, accomplished and spirited, could not possibly want an acquaintance with a future governess like me. But he is in my thoughts all the same. His smile, the cut of his jawline, his hair. How refined his clothing. His singing voice! How I would love to sing with him. But I must put these thoughts out of my head. Flights of fancy will only lead to grief when lingered on too long.

*   *   *

A Duet

I have now seen Mr. Churchill three times in the last four days. He had come to Weymouth to try out the sea bathing, and after his routine morning bathing, he joined us in the assembly rooms of the Royal Hotel. He talked about the waters and how much he enjoyed swimming. I had never learnt and would never have dared go out in one of the bathing machines, but I do enjoy walking along the Bay.

He seemed to share my enjoyment of walking along the water's edge, and he asked what it was that I found so enjoyable. At first, I could only look at him in silence. His eyes were so bright that my mind went blank. I looked away when I realized my hesitation and took a breath to calm my heart. What was wrong with me? I felt like an imbecile, so I quickly cleared my head and told him that I felt the Bay was quite pure, perfectly clear and transparent, a beautiful color. The sands under foot felt soft yet firm, and clean, with no fears of harming one's feet while walking. I enjoyed the gradual declivity of the beach, which allowed an easy walk down and shallow waters to walk in. The Bay was so well sheltered by nature, that entering the water there felt as secure as a bath, and to feel the sands under foot run away with the receding wave was a tranquility that surpasses any pleasure I have ever felt.

Now it was his turn to be silent and look at me. Mr. Dixon and Miss Campbell broke our silent stares with laughter declaring they had never heard me say such a speech before. I confess I am generally a quiet, withdrawn person, but there is something about Mr. Churchill that makes me want to share all that I feel. His own openness seems to influence me. The next two days we met up just the same and we talked about many things; nature, music, drawing, singing and even dancing. The third day he was gone, and his absence was acute. People said that he had just suddenly taken his horse and gone! I felt that I had no one to speak with. Miss Campbell and Mr. Dixon were always engaged in a conversation or a game, so I chose to draw seaside landscapes, but soon fell into daydreaming. I was roused by Miss Campbell laughing as she repeated calling my name. She was asking me where my mind was so occupied, but I couldn't tell her it involved Mr. Churchill bathing in the ocean, his eyes the color of the bluest sky.

When he returned after that one day of absence, I was greatly relieved that he was not gone for good, and he even apologized to *me* for leaving unannounced and explained his trip. He had simply gone to get a haircut. I could see a moderate difference in the look of his hair. He said he planned to return earlier this morning, but as he had traveled down the turnpike road from Dorchester and then descended the hill through the village of Upwey, he took the Narrows road, passing along the seafront. As he continued to near town, he saw Sandsfoot Castle ruins high up on the clay cliffs and decided he had to explore it! But the rain forced him to return before making it all the way up to the cliffs. He hoped to return to explore, and then Mr. Dixon suggested we *all* go out some morning to travel there together. Mr. Churchill readily agreed and Miss Campbell and I were both repressing our great excitement for such a venture!

This evening, Mr. Dixon invited us all for a card party, but after only an hour we were all bored with it and Miss Campbell suggested that I play the piano. Mr. Dixon agreed that I should play for them all and so I did, Corelli and Handel from memory. Then Mr. Churchill found an arrangement of Dibdin and placed it front of me. I was familiar with it and began to play. Instead of walking away, Mr. Dixon stayed by the piano and joined me in the song! I felt as if I was in a dream, for this moment of our voices joining together was what I had wished for. I sang with him, our harmonies perfect and when we were finished, our friends applauded. I didn't dare turn to look at him for fear my complexion would turn rosy. As I stood to leave the pianoforte, Mr. Churchill said quietly that *he* had been hoping for a duet and that he has rarely heard anything so lovely as my playing and singing.

I was so jubilant after that, I found I couldn't say anything at all and I only smiled and tried to breathe slowly. I knew it was just flattery, but why then did it make me feel so happy? Why did I wish he would never stop talking? Why am I still, at this moment, writing by candlelight with my pillow as a desk? Because I am a silly girl with foolish thoughts. I know who I am, where I come from and what I am to be. But while I am here in Weymouth, enjoying the guardianship of the Campbells, why not indulge my flights of fancy? Why not dip my ankles in the sea water and allow the flattery of a most welcome gentleman? This time next year I shall have no chance of this ever again. Now is my time to enjoy.

… After conversing with Miss Campbell, she agrees.

*   *   *

Sandsfoot Castle Expedition

Today was the most exhilarating day of my life! I never knew I would have so much to write in a diary, and until this moment never really understood why women professed that journal writing was so delightful. It was always tedious to me to write about the lessons or needlework or drawing I had done. But now as I write, I agree that reliving all the wonderful moments of the day is very delightful (as long as one has had a day such as this).

The past several days Miss Campbell and I have gone out on morning walks along the seashore. At the women's beach, we splashed through the shallows. Every time I stood still to let the sand run away under my feet with the waves, I thought of Mr. Churchill's bright blue eyes staring into mine. Mr. Dixon and Mr. Churchill have come to call for tea every day and we even went out walking together and had an evening at the theater with the Colonel and Mrs. Campbell, where we all sat together enjoying the music. In the second half, Mr. Churchill came to sit by me to discuss the music. We held the program together and readily debated which songs we most wanted to hear. The music began again and his fingers brushed mine as he closed the program. As we sat and listened, I felt him looking at me and I blushed until I felt warm! After the concert, I could not be comfortable until we were outside and then Mr. Dixon suggested we plan our outing to Sandsfoot Castle. He discussed it with the Colonel. It was decided, we were to go the next day!

Miss Campbell and I woke early this morning. We waited on Mr. Dixon and Mr. Churchill to call on us at the Golden Lion. They were staying at the Crown Inn, not far. A servant announced them and Mr. Dixon first spoke to Colonel Campbell, again for permission to escort Miss Campbell and myself to Sandsfoot Castle ruins. All arrangements had been properly made and he agreed. When the Colonel announced we were to go, my heart leapt and I looked up at Mr. Churchill. He was smiling too, and when my eye caught his, he looked quickly away and sipped his tea. I put on my spencer and bonnet and walked with Miss Campbell outside to discover Mr. Dixon had acquired a four-passenger phaeton with two lovely horses! He assisted Miss Campbell and me into the back seat. He and Mr. Churchill rode in the driver seat.

Mr. Dixon expertly drove the phaeton through the streets and once we were in the country, the horse picked up speed into a gentle trot. I closed my eyes and let the breeze wash over me as the sun glittered orange through my eyelids. When I opened them, Mr. Churchill was turned around looking back. Mr. Dixon slowed the horses so that he could speak. He told us that while having breakfast at the Crown Inn, he heard someone mention a dance to be held soon at the Royal Hotel, in just a few days! He promised to find out more about it, for it would be wonderful if we all met up there. I smiled, trying not to show too much elation, though I felt my cheeks redden when Mr. Churchill looked at me. Miss Campbell, always happy to speak for me, said she would be very happy if there was to be a dance, for it has been ages since we attended a ball or even an evening dance.

"Jane usually plays if we dance at our home, though she is a lovely dancer."

Mr. Churchill said, "I am sure she is. And if she dances half as well as she plays, she will be engaged the entire evening, I'm sure."

I told him not to tease me, and he looked confused and ensured me that he wasn't. Then Mr. Dixon kicked up the horses as we were going up a hill. Very soon we were at the top of the cliffs and the Sandsfoot ruins came into view! I had seen it from a distance, but up-close the structure was breathtaking. Mr. Dixon drove the phaeton onto the flat plateau and, while he was hitching the horses, Mr. Churchill assisted us down and I felt his hand in mine for the first time. We all explored the outside of the large castle together, and I imagined what it might have looked like in its full glory, with its high curved windows on the second story of the blockhouse and the large curved gun platform that is clearly falling into the sea below.

We wandered inside through an opening, as all the doors were gone and much of the stone had fallen or been removed long ago. I stopped to take off my bonnet, and Mr. Dixon and Miss Campbell suddenly disappeared down a passage. I could hear Mr. Dixon talking about the history of the castle, made of Portland stone and Ashlar facings that had been taken for the construction of the Weymouth Bridge, etc. Mr. Churchill, however, didn't follow them or seem to mind that we were alone, and he quietly asked me if I was imagining how grand it all must have been two hundred years ago. We walked and envisioned a fanciful history together, inventing stories of men living there and what each room and stairwell might have been for. We peeked out an old archway to look down the cliffs at the sea below, and then we were suddenly silent. We stood together in the archway, the rush of the crashing waves on one side and the empty stillness on the other. We were completely alone and suddenly we were very aware of it. I knew I shouldn't look, but Frank Churchill's eyes were so blue. I just stared into them until there was nothing else. He reached forward and moved some fallen hair out of my face and behind my ear. And this was the most amazing moment! He took my hands in his suddenly and whispered to me, "Miss Fairfax, you are the loveliest creature I have ever beheld. I hope that... I desire that you will promise me the first dance at the Royal Hotel, for the only thing that could give me more pleasure than singing with you would be to dance with you. Will you agree?"

I nodded my head and unknowingly squeezed his hands in mine, only realizing I had done it when he squeezed back. He stepped closer to me and I had to lift my chin to see him. He leaned down closer and he whispered, "Miss Fairfax."

I thought he was going to kiss me and I started to panic! I think it was panic. My heart raced so hard and my fingertips were numb and my head became light. But then we heard Mr. Dixon's voice talking about Portland Castle that was across the harbor and Mr. Churchill pulled away. They came around the corner then and joined us, looking through the archway to the sea. We all went back to the phaeton and Mr. Dixon unpacked a lovely picnic lunch for us. As we sat in the shade of the ruins, I listened to them talk about this and that. Miss Campbell talked about the dance and Mr. Dixon about how the cliffs by the sea reminded him of Ireland. I only half listened, however, as my mind was wandering back to that moment in the arch and what might have happened if we had not been interrupted. I fantasized about Mr. Churchill kissing me, embracing me, pressing me against the stone ruins, holding my hands above my head as he... well, I was pulled out of my reverie by Mr. Churchill suggesting how exhilarating it would be to go sailing, since the weather was so fine. That got the men into talking about sailing and what would be the best type of ship to take out and how grand a water party would be.

I listened, understanding now that everything Mr. Churchill was about was in order to include me in a party with him. The trip home was lovely, and he assisted me out of the phaeton once more, this time squeezing my hand before letting go. After our farewells, we rested in the drawing room until dinner and Mrs. Campbell excitedly told us there *would* be a dance at the Royal Hotel the next Saturday evening, if we would be interested in going! It was soon all secured that we would go and four days seemed like a lifetime away. But I would be dancing with Mr. Churchill.

That he had an affection for me was certain, that I felt great fondness for him was very certain. But I had to check myself. He is from a wealthy family, I have nothing. I do not pretend that any young man of fortune could ever look upon me seriously. I have been warned by Mrs. Campbell and my governess about the flirtations and flattery of men who have no true intentions and only mischief in their minds. I know this. And yet... I long to hear Frank Churchill whisper my name once more. If I am his object of mischief, I shall revel in it and endeavor to protect myself from those feelings of heartbreak which threaten to arise when I think of his leaving and never seeing him again.

*   *   *

The Dance at the Royal

A few dull days have gone by with only the excitement of a dance at the Royal to get us though. Though I was in nervous trepidation during the wait, because Mr. Churchill was called away to London, (something to do with an ailing Aunt) and promised to return by Saturday. On Saturday afternoon, there was still no word if he was returned or not, for Mr. Dixon was over and he had not seen nor heard from him. We went to the dance and I looked all around the beautiful rooms of the Royal Hotel, but could not see him. Mr. Dixon kindly asked to take Miss Campbell away for the first set, and just as I was beginning to despair, there he was. As fine as ever, smartly dressed and grinning with an air of secretly knowing something. He bowed and asked for the dance. We joined the others in the set and Miss Campbell caught my eye with a smile. The music began and we moved easily through the dance, his hands holding mine. I asked Mr. Churchill about his expression, and he only replied that he was very pleased to see that I had not found another partner for the dance. "You waited for me."

"We had an engagement. I couldn't have stood up with another when you had reserved the first dance, even if you had not been here." I moved past him and joined him again on the other side of the line.

"So, had I not even come tonight, you would not have danced?" He grinned widely.

"Not the first set, no."

"Miss Fairfax, I am beginning to think you are the sweetest and most angelic woman I shall ever know. I am trying to find a fault with you and I simply cannot!"

My thoughts went immediately to my lack of any inheritance but I said,

"Perhaps accepting all this flattery is a fault."

He paused at that, not sure if I meant to silence him, but I couldn't help smile and blush. He held my hand as we danced through the center of the group and he said, "If I am to be a part of any creation of fault in you, then I shall retreat, though I feel my praise for you is truth and not flattery. I shall refrain from speaking. How my thoughts are engaged towards you shall be my business."

We faced each other as the dance ended and bowed. He looked at me so warmly then that I wished he would speak more and tell me all that he felt. We were forced to move away from the floor and Mr. Dixon and Miss Campbell joined us. Mr. Dixon asked Mr. Churchill if he'd told me yet.

"Not yet," he replied. "Did you tell Miss Campbell?"

"Not a word yet," said Mr. Dixon.

Miss Campbell and I looked at each other quizzically, and she demanded to know what it was they hadn't told us yet. Mr. Dixon explained that they had chartered a sailing boat for Monday before tea to go out into the bay!

"A sailing party!" Miss Campbell exclaimed, and Mr. Churchill looked at me earnestly.

"You will come, Miss Fairfax?"

"Only so long as Colonel Campbell approves."

"We shall go address him at once." And Mr. Dixon and Churchill were off.

Miss Campbell expressed how excited she was to be going out on a boat and how Mr. Dixon and Mr. Churchill were paying quite a bit of attention towards us.

"I do not think I have ever seen two men such in love."

"Don't be silly. I mean, I believe Mr. Dixon is truly attached to you, of course. But Mr. Churchill is only…"

I was going to say he was only having a bit of fun, when another gentleman approached and asked me for the honor of the next dance. Well, I had no reason to refuse him, and he led me to the floor. He was a kind chap and danced well. We talked a little about where we were from and how we enjoyed Weymouth. At the end of the dance, I noticed Mr. Churchill watching. I don't know why, but I felt a small pang of guilt. I had done nothing wrong, but it felt wrong to be dancing with someone else while he was there. I returned to Miss Campbell and then Mr. Dixon asked me to dance and Miss Campbell joined with Mr. Churchill.

After the lively dance, I sat to rest for a moment while Miss Campbell went to speak to her mother. Looking around at the splendor of the room, I decided to explore the different rooms of the Royal before the next set.

After only a moment of exploring, I found Mr. Dixon and Mr. Churchill talking quietly by a window. I heard my name mentioned. They hadn't seen me, so I stood around the corner. I listened. I couldn't help it.

Mr. Dixon was telling Mr. Churchill my story, as I'm sure Miss Campbell would have told him.

"Miss Jane Fairfax is an orphan with no siblings. Her Lieutenant father died abroad and her mother died soon after. She was raised in Highbury, as you know, by her aunt and grandmother, Mrs. and Miss Bates. At nine years old, she went to live with Colonel Campbell; he was a great friend of her father's."

"And she is meant to live on her own? Is she not provided for?" Mr. Churchill said this with much concern, though I didn't dare try to look at his face.

"She has no inheritance. She was brought up to be a governess, though the Colonel will care for her, I'm sure, until she secures a position. Miss Campbell says she is much loved, like a daughter to the Campbells."

"Of course," was all Mr. Churchill said, but I wondered if he would ever ask me to dance again.

Distressed, I sat back down. How had he not heard this until now? Was he courting me, believing I had a greater fortune? Was he paying me all this attention, not knowing I was penniless? I worried he would be upset when he came back and would not wish to speak to me. And indeed, when he returned to the dance, he did look grave. But then he saw me. I must have been looking at him earnestly. He smiled brightly and rushed over to ask for the next dance, which would be the last of the evening. I was hesitant, but reminded myself to have fun while I could and determined to not think about the future.

A waltz began and Mr. Churchill took my hand. He

squeezed it gently and that roused me. We began the dance and he asked me what I was thinking of, looking so downcast. I told him I was not downcast at all, and I was only thinking that I should be perfectly happy this evening. He smiled, but it was a sad smile. And we danced for a moment, I believe, both feeling the loss of each other.

Finally, he said in nearly a whisper, "Miss Fairfax, I know you do not like to hear me tell you the wonderful things I have to say about you, but I must tell you that you are in my thoughts almost always. I do not wish to distress you, but let us agree that tonight, we shall be determined to enjoy our time together. For tonight, we shall not be bound by any confines. Let us waltz together as if this was the last dance."

"It is the last dance." I said rationally. But I perfectly understood what he was saying. We had no future, but we still wanted to be together, and at least for tonight, we could pretend. I wanted nothing more. I quickly continued with, "And nothing you have to say will distress me this evening. I am determined that we shall enjoy it, as long as we are together."

His hands tightened around mine, and as we danced he looked at me as I thought no man would ever look at me. As I danced, I pretended I was a rich countess and he was my betrothed. I held my head up and did not blush as we looked at each other. We took hands over and over, weaving through the other couples in the dance, hardly knowing there were other people in the room. After the dance, we bowed, and as he led me off the floor he leaned close and whispered in my ear.

"Please meet me outside. I wish to speak with you."

He bowed and walked away, leaving me in shock. Miss Campbell came over and asked if I was feeling alright. I gathered myself and said yes, I just needed some air. She said she would come with me, but I told her I would be fine. Luckily, Mr. Dixon came over, then took Miss Campbell away to her mother and father. I headed to the doors that led outside, and as it was a brisk evening, only a few people stood there talking. I walked beyond the courtyard, onto the grass to look out at the moon. I wondered what I was doing there, and what I expected. Was I really going to risk my reputation by staying out any longer? I turned to go back in, and there was Mr. Churchill. My heart skipped a beat.

The others had gone in, and he was hidden from view by a tall topiary by the door. I slowly approached him, fear growing in me. My stomach tightened as he reached out and took my hands.

"Miss Fairfax, you came. It means the world to me. I must tell you what is in my heart. I know we haven't much time."

My hands actually went numb as he spoke. He held them and lifted them up to his chest. I could feel his heart racing beneath his waistcoat.

He said, "Please allow me to tell you that on our first acquaintance, I was taken with you. I wanted to know everything about you. You have, every day, made me feel even more for you. You do not wish to hear flattery, but I must tell you that you are the most stunning, accomplished, kind, gentle, perfect woman I have ever known. I wanted you to know this before I go away tomorrow."

I wanted to tell him how I felt as well, but I couldn't say anything at all. I was so happy! But then, what? He was going away?

I said, "Going away? Why? I thought we were planning a sailing party? What has changed?"

He looked away then, so desperate, so distressed. He lifted my hands up and kissed them. I understood his distress. He cared about me, but could never marry me. He could not risk all he had by marrying a penniless girl. He did not want me to be upset when he withdrew his attentions. He did not want me to assume his intentions were marriage, but he did not want me to think he was a scoundrel either. Though I wanted to cry, I instead reminded him of our resolution,

"Mr. Churchill, remember our promise to enjoy tonight, if tonight is all we have."

He pulled me suddenly towards him, his hand on the small of my back, and he kissed me. A warm, passionate kiss. He stopped and looked at me with wide surprised eyes, clearly shocked that he had given in to such an impulse. I did not wish for him to stop, so I lifted my chin and kissed him again. He let out a small moan, and I felt a pleasure, like a shock, move up through my body. I grabbed onto the collar of his jacket and kissed him harder, and he pressed his hand into my back, lifting me up. We broke off the kiss and leaned our foreheads together, breathing hard.

"Oh how I wish…" he said.

Oh how I wish. How I wish my parents hadn't died, how I wish I had a dowry, how I wish I had never met Mr. Frank Churchill! I pulled away and fought back the tears in my eyes.

I said, "It stops now. No more. My heart can take no more."

And I left him. I went inside and found the Campbells. The Colonel looked at me and became concerned. "My dear, are you well? You look pale."

"I was just outside… I needed air. It was a bit chilly after a moment, that's all."

He decided that it was time to say goodbyes and head to the carriage. Mr. Dixon walked Miss Campbell to the outside and I took Colonel Campbell's arm. Mr. Churchill was in the hall and he bowed as we passed. I did not look up, though I could feel his gaze. I was silent during the carriage ride home, but once I was in bed, I cried. Then I started writing, and here we are. Just my pen and my thoughts that won't let me sleep. I am beginning to wonder about Mr. Churchill's intentions now. I made all those excuses for him at the party, but why, when earlier in the evening he was so keen to plan a sailing party, would he suddenly, after speaking with Mr. Dixon about me, choose to leave Weymouth? Just to avoid me? Why would he risk my reputation by asking me to come outside with him alone? And to kiss me! Regardless of how much I enjoyed it, he did it, knowing full well he would not propose. Am I deceived in his character? Was he, as Mrs. Campbell and my governess warned me against, a man with mischievous intentions?

And what of my behavior? I had walked alone with him at Sandsfoot. I flirted and danced with him, showing no restraint. I had joined him outside, alone when he asked me to. I kissed him back. How have my actions shown my character to him? What must he think of me? Perhaps he thinks I am a fortune hunter? That is why he goes away? I cannot think of it any longer, I must go to sleep. I have no more in me, my tears are dried out.

*   *   *

Near Death

They are engaged! Just like that, love has found my friend and she will soon be hereafter called Mrs. Dixon. Oh, my dear happy friend is so excited to see Ireland!

But let me go back to the morning after the dance. I slept long the day after the dance, as was to be expected, but I did not want to go out, even when Miss Campbell urged me to accompany her. I simply hadn't the energy or desire to see anything in Weymouth.

"It looks like rain," I said, looking out the window at the clear blue sky. Miss Campbell then pressed me for why I was down and quickly guessed it was because of Mr. Churchill. I was adamant that I had no expectations. We were only acquaintances and only appeared to be more than friends because we were always with her and Mr. Dixon. I turned the subject back to her and she told me how gentlemanly Mr. Dixon had been at the dance, dancing twice with her, once with me, and never with anyone else. He had apparently been speaking with the Colonel for some time.

"I am certain, certain he will ask me today! So I NEED you to come out with me today so that he and I might be alone together. Please?"

She begged, I relented. We went out and Mr. Dixon met us out on our walk. He took his place beside her and I walked back a bit. And then, it started to rain! Out of the blue, clouds rolled in from the ocean, and rain poured down on all of us. We rushed to find shelter in a small gazebo off the beach. Alone, slightly damp, and surrounded by the rushing sound of the rain and the waves beating the shore, there was no better opportunity for Mr. Dixon. He proposed, Miss Campbell accepted, and that was settled. Miss Campbell was the happiest I had ever seen her, and I was happy for her, though I could not lift my spirits to what they should be. I was again upset with Mr. Churchill for making me the miserable creature I was, yet I reminded myself that I knew this was to be the only outcome of opening my heart.

Luckily, it rained the next few days, so we did not have the chance to go out. Mr. Dixon came for breakfast and tea each day, and I had to sit in the room as a chaperone with him and Miss Campbell, or else Mrs. Campbell would have to sit in. Though they were engaged, the Colonel still did not think it proper for them to be alone. I just wanted to be in my room. I felt childish and idiotic for pining over Mr. Churchill, re-living our kisses over and over in my mind, and then becoming angry with myself for letting such fancy takeover. It seemed that Mr. Dixon and Miss Campbell knew there was some tension, for they hardly ever mentioned him.

Mr. Dixon did speak of Mr. Churchill once, telling Miss Campbell that on the evening of the dance, Frank had received word that he must go home to his sick aunt again to help remove her to London. I wasn't sure if I believed that. Mr. Dixon also said that as soon as he returned, we would all go out sailing as promised. I gave him a very little smile, trying not to show displeasure in the notion of his returning and having to pretend he was nothing to me. If he returned and was cold, I just didn't think I could bear it! But a week passed with no word of him returning. I ventured outside again for morning walks on the beach and afternoon outings into town.

Mr. Dixon and Miss Campbell were very happy to have me chaperone them again on long walks into the countryside or along the bay. They walked closer together and I walked a little further back so that they might have private conversations. I was certain that Frank Churchill had quitted Weymouth and would not return, having escaped the dangers of a flirtatious, penniless, kissing seductress, which is what I was sure he thought I was.

The next week was sunny every day. Mr. Dixon

decided not to wait any longer, and we should go on our sailing excursion once he could make arrangements. It was settled that we would go on Thursday.

Frank Churchill returned to Weymouth on Wednesday. Imagine my surprise when Thursday morning, we were all gathered at the marina, when Mr. Dixon arrives with Mr. Churchill! I was shocked. I almost let out an audible gasp! Mr. Dixon said something about the fortuitous timing of his return and everyone welcomed him warmly. I could not look at him or say a word. I hardly knew what I was doing as we boarded the vessel and found our seats. The sailing master untied the ship. Miss Campbell was waving goodbye to the Colonel and Mrs. Campbell on the shore, Mr. Dixon was smiling happily, and Mr. Churchill was staring at me.

I kept my eyes out on the horizon as we sailed through the bay. I involuntarily glanced at him and he opened his mouth to speak, but said nothing. He looked remarkably well. Mr. Dixon pointed out Sandsfoot Castle as we passed. I am sure I blushed. Mr. Dixon and the soon-to-be-Mrs. Dixon moved to the bow of the sailboat to look out towards the ocean. This is when Mr. Churchill came to sit by me. Our conversation went like this,

"Miss Fairfax, how are you? I long to know what you have been doing this past week. I have been assisting my aunt moving from Enscombe to London, to the doctors there. She is ill you see, but she is always ill, so we believe she is healthy as an ox and only enjoys travelling."

I didn't respond to his light-hearted joke. I only said that the weather had been rainy. I was cold to him, unresponsive, and he seemed confused and upset. I didn't want to show him that I was hurt by his leaving or give any kind of encouragement that I would repeat our indiscretions. But I was mostly protecting my heart, for I knew if I looked into his eyes again I would be lost.

He tried again, pointing out some of the sights and naming some of the birds. We drew close to the inlet and the wind picked up. Then he leaned towards me and tried to take my hand in his! I pulled away and would not look at him or speak. My mind was too full.

Finally, he said, "Miss Fairfax, please forgive me. Please do not reproach me for my indiscretions. I was wrong to treat you so. My passions took control of me during those weeks together. I hold you in the highest honor and dread to consider what you must think of me. Please tell me we are still friends."

At this I turned, for I could not be silent on that speech. "I am afraid we cannot be friends, Mr. Churchill. I do not think I shall ever be safe in your presence. Had I known you were coming today, I should not have come."

He looked stunned and shaken. He stammered, "But, Miss Fairfax..."

I continued, "You have become far too dear to me ever to be considered only a friend, and I could never meet with you as only an acquaintance. I shall always be in danger of wishing to be close to you, see the passion in your eyes, wanting to hear your lovely whispering voice, and feel your hands holding mine. We cannot continue in this way. I am simply not strong enough to pretend that I feel nothing for you. It will be better that our acquaintance end and that we see each other no more."

I stood up and moved towards the bow. I let the wind carry the tears from my eyes. I stood there for some time, not knowing what affect my speech had on Mr. Churchill, for he was silent. We were approaching the bay inlet where the wide ocean loomed. A sudden wind gust rushed over the boat and a sail tore away. The boom swung on me before I knew there was even a danger! My back was hit and my feet slipped out from beneath me. I saw the water below as I fell over the boat, and then I was caught! Mr. Dixon had grabbed hold of the back of my habit and in an instant pulled me back on board. Everything became quite a blur, but I remember Miss Campbell screaming and hugging me, while a blanket was put around my shoulders and I was led back to the seats, and everyone was gathered around me. I assured everyone that I was alright, but the boat was turned and we headed back to Weymouth. I was offered food and drink. I took a little wine, and it was Mr. Churchill handing it to me. He was pale and said not a word. I felt terrible for speaking to him the way I did and I thanked him most heartily for the wine. I thanked Mr. Dixon a dozen times, as it became more and more clear to me that he had saved my life.

A half an hour later we neared the marina and Mr. Dixon asked Miss Campbell for advice on what to do. She said someone must run to tell the Colonel so that he might send the carriage to take Jane home and call for a doctor. I really did not like all this fuss being made. I really was not hurt, and could have easily made the walk home, but I did not fight them. Mr. Churchill volunteered, and before the boat was tied to the dock, he had leaped off and started running. I watched him run, fast and strong, without any thought of what the people he passed may have thought. Here was no man looking for mischief, here was no unfeeling man. He was running, and he was running for me.

My heart ached. I did not want to care for him. The carriage soon pulled up with the Colonel and I was led slowly and lifted gently into it. Miss Campbell boarded with me, and as the carriage drove away, I saw Mr. Dixon turn to the sailing master and start yelling at him. We reached home and I saw Mr. Churchill waiting outside with the doctor. As I was assisted out of the carriage, I caught Mr. Churchill's eye and nodded with a little smile to show my gratitude for his efforts in informing the Colonel. He held his palms together, his fingers on his lips and stood watching as the Colonel and the doctor followed me inside. I was soon laid in my bed, and the doctor looked at my back and checked my breathing and heart. He said I might be sore a day or two, and that rest would dispel the shock. I told the Colonel that Mr. Dixon had saved me from being thrown from the boat, but he already knew the whole story from Mr. Churchill. And now I must rest, for today I might have died, and that has me thinking more about life.

*   *   *

Back from the Brink

It has now been five days since the sailing incident. Miss Campbell sat with me in my room for two days, and Mr. Dixon visited on the third morning when I was told I could venture down to the drawing room. Both of them seemed very cautious as to *not* mention Mr. Churchill. I wondered if he had gone away again, but didn't dare ask. Finally, at tea, Miss Campbell asked me if I was strong enough for a card party. I said that I felt fine and would be willing to go out for walk on the beach if they would let me. Even after my speech to Mr. Churchill, I still longed to see him and I had hoped he might come visit me. That afternoon, several people did come over for cards, but Mr. Churchill was not among them. I had to assume that he was respecting my wishes of no longer being an acquaintance, and I was very sorry for it. I could hide it from everyone else, but not from myself. I loved

Frank Churchill. I missed him and longed to feel his hands on mine, to feel him holding me, kissing me, to feel his breath and his heartbeat racing. Just to see him again. That is all I wanted. Just to see him so that he would know I did not bear him any ill will.

When the card games were done and we moved into the sitting room, I prepared the coffee despite protests from the others that I should be resting. I assured them that I was just fine when a low voice said, "You are stronger than most, Miss Fairfax." I looked up and Mr. Churchill stood before me. I dropped the empty cup in my hand and Frank picked it up.

He smiled widely and said he would take that cup, please. I poured the coffee and he stepped to the side as other gentlemen entered. Mr. Dixon quickly sat himself by Miss Campbell, and after the coffee was served, I looked around. Mr. Churchill was sitting near the fire, with no seats near him. I sat by the window and watched him. He did not seem uneasy, but rather steady. He talked and laughed with the others and twice caught me looking at him. I determined not to catch his eyes again. I heard several people talk of Mr. Dixon's amazing rescue of myself, and that I had come so close to being lost in the rough waters. I raised my cup and announced to the room a toast, to Mr. Dixon for his quick-thinking in pulling me back from the brink. Everyone chanted, 'Back from the brink! Here, here!'

Mr. Churchill patted his friend on the back and shook his hand as Mr. Dixon pleaded that it was just luck that he happened to walk back from the bow at that very moment. He declared that I was safe, and that was all that mattered. Mr. Churchill looked at me then, but I was looking away, pretending not to notice. He stood and walked over and then sat in front of me by the window!

He said quietly, "I promise I will not take any more of your time, Miss Fairfax. I came only to say that I am exceedingly happy you are looking so well."

I did not look into his eyes; my eyes were instead drawn to his lips, and I watched them as he spoke, imagining them on my lips again.

He continued, "And I wish that, I mean, I hope that, in time, we may be able to continue our acquaintance, under the conditions you so clearly specified."

I was brought out of my imaginings by this veiled speech and blurted, "What?"

Then Miss Campbell and others of our circle joined us by the window. They began talking of something inconsequential, and Mr. Churchill left. I worked very hard not to follow him with my eyes. As the other ladies talked, I was lost in thought about what he might mean. What conditions had I specified? I had told him we could not continue our acquaintance because I would not be able to bear being nothing to him. Did he mean that he hoped we might, in time, be able to remain as friends? Did he mean that he intended to rekindle those feelings which I told him I had to repress? Why was he doing this to me?!

I suddenly stood up, overcome with emotion, and made my excuses that I needed to rest. I walked through the house to the stairs and I stopped with a gasp. Mr. Churchill was standing at the window near the entrance. He must have heard me because he turned then and we found ourselves alone in the foyer. We stared at each other in surprise for a moment, and then he walked briskly over to me and grasped my hands. He led me quickly around the corner, into the passage behind the stairs, and I did not protest, as I was lightheaded, and excited, and afraid, all at once.

The only light was from a dim candle just outside the passage, and his blue eyes glowed in the light. He bit his lip as he looked at me. and leaned towards me as if he was going to kiss me. He hesitated and said,

"Miss Fairfax, I know you do not wish to speak to me. You have every right to have believed me insincere after leaving town so often without proper communication to you. I was hasty, I was unguarded, and I was fearful, but never insincere. You have held my heart from the moment I first saw you singing at the piano and I cannot let our… friendship end without telling you how this whole event had affected me. I must tell you, when you nearly were dashed from the boat, I had never before been so frightened in all my life. You seemed so calm, and I was completely undone. The thought of having almost lost you, it bears no clarification. If ever I was uncertain of my desires, if ever I had reservations or faltering confidence, due in part to my own intolerable family situation, those doubts are gone now. The thought of you not in the world is so terrible to me, and the thought of you not in my life is unbearable. There is, and never will be, anyone for me but you, and I must know if would have me…"

I had been watching his lips as he spoke, and I finally couldn't resist any longer. I stepped closer and kissed him. He wrapped his arms around me in a warm embrace, pulling me close, and for a moment I was lost in a dream. But he pulled away, breathless, and became anxious.

"My dear, Miss Fairfax, please I must tell you all. My family would object, well, mainly my Aunt, and until I am able to change that situation, we would have to maintain secrecy. But I promise it will not be too long. I will do everything in my power to marry you as soon as I can. Please say you will marry me, though it must be a secret engagement. Tell me you will wait for me. Tell me I shall be happy forever."

I was being proposed to! By a man I loved! By a man who would save me from a lifetime of servitude and sorrow. Waiting would be nothing, delaying taking a position as a governess would not be a problem with the Campbells, and with all the attention on Miss Campbell and Mr. Dixon's wedding, secrecy would be easy.

I told him nothing would bring me more joy than to accept, if he would only promise that we might correspond during any lengthy absence from each other, and that he would come to see me as often as would appear prudent. He stared at me in disbelief and in joy. He kissed me again and I pressed myself against him as his arms wrapped around me. My hands found themselves around his back and lowering to his firm bum.

He drew in a sharp breath and exclaimed, "Oh, Miss Fairfax!" He had this image of me as an angel, proper and demure. But if he only knew my fantasies, *he* would blush.

I smiled at him as innocently as I could and said, "I expect that we shall find ways to be together during our engagement that will bring us much pleasure."

His mouth agape, I left him then, quietly moving from under the stairs to the second level and entering my bedroom. I threw myself on the bed and laughed into my pillow, until I picked up this diary and now I have related the whole of the evening.

$$*\qquad\qquad *\qquad\qquad *$$

Dear Diary,

The wedding is over and Mr. and *Mrs. Dixon* are off to Ireland! Funny calling my dear friend by the name of Mrs. Dixon, now. Winter is coming, and I hope that her first impressions of her new home are not dampened by the cold and snow. The Colonel and Mrs. Campbell expect to be able to visit them in the spring, and though I too would enjoy seeing Ireland, I have other plans. Spring and summer in Highbury will be just the excuse I need to have more freedom to see Frank Churchill, as his father still lives there. And I will be able to extend my delay in seeking a position as a governess at least until the Campbell's return. At one-and-twenty, I know I have already delayed my start, but the Campbells do not seem to mind in the least, and Mrs. Campbell has even told me that with her daughter gone, she couldn't possibly do without me for some time.

I have not been well these past few weeks, nor have I been able to see Frank since our last day together at the Dixon's wedding in Weymouth. Though we have been able to correspond secretly, as I make it my daily duty to receive the post for the Campbells. Frank's letters are generally short, but full of promises and devotion and reminders of wonderful moments between ourselves. His letter today reminded me of our second outing to Sandsfoot Castle, a few days before the wedding.

He had written, "I found myself today wishing we were back at Sandsfoot, hidden away in our own little corner of rapture, where the strength of the waves crashing against the cliffs was nothing to my beating heart as you kissed me so. Oh, that we were back in Sandsfoot, upon the soft grass and stone walls."

Mild words for what we had experienced there. I shall write about it now, as I have so terribly neglected writing in my diary and have only been using it to store letters.

Mr. Churchill, Mr. Dixon, Miss Campbell and I decided to see Sandsfoot one more time before the wedding. After that, we would be going home to London, and then the Dixons would continue on to Ireland. I was very aware that Mr. Churchill and I only had these last moments before leaving Weymouth, and we would possibly not see each other for a very long time. Once we reached Sandsfoot ruins, we split off into pairs, with Mr. Dixon and Miss Campbell starting off exploring the outside, and Mr. Churchill and I moving inside. We explored the nooks and crannies, literally searching for a place we could hide ourselves away. Being secretly engaged instead of openly engaged meant that people watched you less, but the excitement of not being caught was all the greater.

We found a small circular stone alcove that perhaps once housed a stairwell up to the barbican. Totally enclosed, save one small opening, we hid inside, turned to each other, and kissed, for we had been aching for each other. Over the course of several weeks, every secret glance and every clandestine touch made me mad with desire, and now, being truly alone, I allowed him to press himself against me with the gray stone walls at my back. I held his collar, which I loved to do, and held my mouth open as his tongue caressed my lips. Then he leaned down to kiss my neck. My lips brushed his ear, and I whispered his name as I ran my hand teasingly over his leg. His hands ran down my back as he grasped my backside, pulling me even closer to him.

I bit his ear a little, and his moans encouraged me to be a little more rough with him. I tugged at his hair and bit gently on his bottom lip. He went wild for it and grasped my hands, pulling them up, crossed over my head. Pressing me against the stone wall, he held my hands up and kissed me with his whole mouth. I had fantasized about this moment, and my body shook with excitement! I held my hands crossed at the wrists, over my head, as his hands slid down my arms to my breast.

He unbuttoned my spencer jacket, which fell open, revealing my low cut muslin, and he kissed my chest running his fingers over the edging of my dress. I stood still as he kneeled down to kiss my breasts. I could feel his lips even through the layers of material, and his hands slowly slipped down my waist and thighs. My hands came down to run through his hair, and soon I kneeled as well, where his lips moved from my breast to my mouth, and back again.

The more we touched each other, the more wild we became. We knew this would be our last chance for many months to be together, and soon we were laying on the ground, where the grass and moss had taken over the flooring. He pressed himself on top of me, and though I had several layers of underclothes, they were all delicate and thin and I could feel him intimately. His fingers pulled my dress front down and his face pressed between my bosoms. He was able to remove one of my breasts from the short stay, and when he ran his tongue over me, my entire body arched up towards him in pleasure. With his pelvis pressed into mine, I could feel his arousal through our thin clothes, moving ever so slightly up and down. I felt him touch a part of me that sent a spasm of pleasure through my body. He moved my hips to align with him so that I would feel that pleasure with every thrust. The movement became faster and the pleasure was growing inside me. I ached to feel him more deeply. I knew we understood each other, that we would wait to consummate our marriage. However, those concerns did not enter my head as I pulled up my dress and petticoat to feel him between my bare legs. His soft trousers rubbed against my bare skin (as of course, I worn no bloomers) and he seemed nearly mad with desire.

His movement paired with the pleasure of his tongue

on my breast sent me into spasms of ecstasy. He kissed me on the lips again as he slowed his rhythm. He sat up and ran his hands up and down my bare legs, above the stockings. His fingers teased between my legs and I arched up to them, yearning to feel him inside me. I sat up and reached for his trouser buttons, his fingers tickling me, his lips once again on mine.

But we heard voices. They were muted and distant, but inside the ruins no less. We looked at each other in desperate dismay, both fearful of being discovered and crestfallen in having to stop.

I fixed the top of my dress and adjusted my stay, as Frank re-tied his loosened cravat and breathed deeply to calm himself down. I buttoned my spencer jacket and he straightened his waistcoat.

We paused and listened. The voices were faint, then they passed by. Mr. Dixon and Miss Campbell had not discovered our hidden alcove.

"Jane," Frank started, "If we had more time… but, no, we must stop now or we may go too far."

"You are right, of course, but the thought of not touching you for so long… I cannot bear it."

He kissed me again and I slid up onto his lap.

He said, "We shall see each other soon in Highbury, and there we shall have freedoms and time together to make us very unsafe."

I imagined us alone in a room of my Aunt's house, on a tufted couch, wearing no clothes and Frank kissing my entire body. Fantasies must have run through both our heads, because I felt him rise again under me. I wiggled a little over him and I knew I could not leave so unsatisfied.

I pushed him down into the grass, kneeled over him, and whispered in his ear, "I must have you now." I sucked on his lip as I unbuttoned his trouser fall and lifted his shirt. His breathing became heavy as he pulled up my dress and petticoat. As I lowered myself over him, I was quivering with desire. I slid down on him and we both gasped. We moved together slowly, and building speed, our hips pushed against one another and pleasure wracked over my entire body.

He sat up and embraced me, kissing my neck and ears and lips. I wrapped my legs around him and we pulsed together, nothing in our thoughts but the pleasure we brought each other, wishing it would never end. I whispered in his ear as pleasure built up inside me.

"Frank! Don't stop!"

My legs shook. Every muscle contracted. My hands were numb. All thought was gone as my mind was exploding in pleasure. I gasped, and wanted to cry out, but I gritted my teeth and only quietly moaned, then whispered Frank's name over and over.

Finally, we knew we had to stop. Frank slowly pulled away.

He stood, and after buttoning and straightening his clothes, he assisted me up.

"My god, you're wonderful," he said. "You are more amazing than I ever could have dreamed! How is a man like me to be worthy of such perfection?"

I smiled, adjusting my petticoat and stockings. He replaced a few pins in my hair and I brushed some clover from his. He kissed me one more time, gently, and when we had recovered ourselves, we ventured back out and walked along the outside of the ruins, allowing the sea wind to blow through our hair and redden our faces. At least, that was the excuse we all four of us used once we reunited at the phaeton.

We had a short lunch near the edge of the cliffs and talked about the wedding plans for the next day before riding out. Because they were engaged, Mr. Dixon and Miss Campbell now sat together in the front, while Mr. Churchill and I were obliged to sit in the back. That suited us just fine, as we could talk about what we wished while our hips touched, and I could hold his arm along the bumpy roads.

After the wedding, we said goodbye, he kissed my hand and I passed him a note- the first of our secret correspondence- with instructions on how to address his letters. He watched my carriage drive out all the way down the road, until I could no longer see him.

So now I must wait alone at the Colonel's home until the invitation to visit Ireland arrives, and I must give my excuses of not accompanying them. It was Mr. Churchill's suggestion to go to Highbury and live with my aunt and grandmother when the Campbells go to Ireland, so that we might have many more opportunities to be together under the unsuspicious eyes and negligible supervision of the Bates. I do hope our engagement does not have to be too long, but knowing Frank (how dear that name is to me now) it shall not be uneventful.

Author Bio

A. L. Ady is a woman of particular tastes and refined sensibilities. When she is not sipping tea in the garden reading a Jane Austen novel, she can found curled up in a wingback chair with a laptop, drinking iced coffee and writing regency romance.

18464163R00078

Made in the USA
San Bernardino, CA
20 December 2018